HUNTER'S HEART

Daughters of Elysium—Book One

S. M. SHADOW

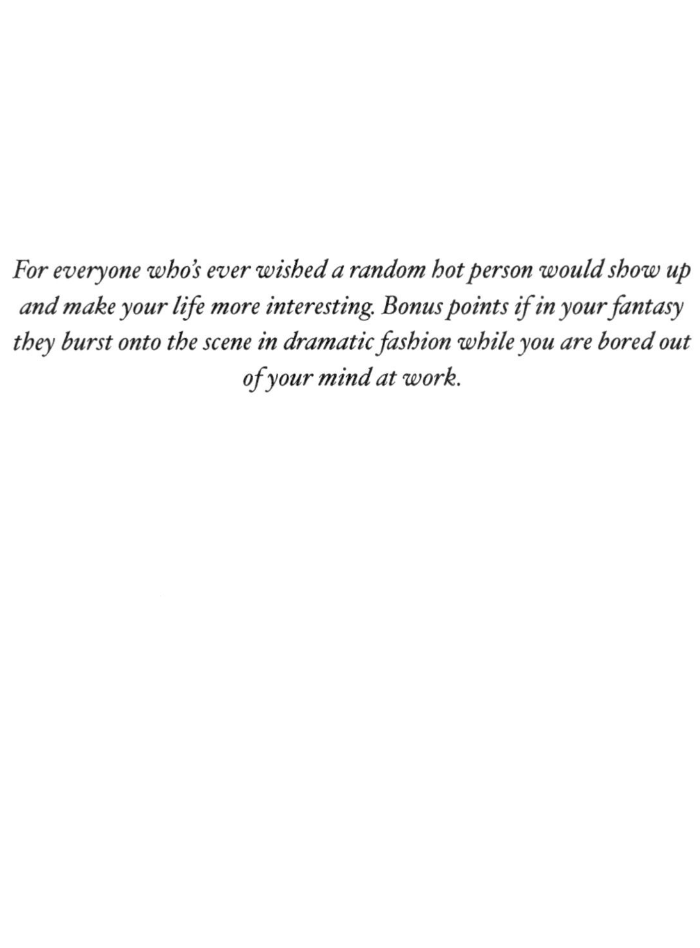

For everyone who's ever wished a random hot person would show up and make your life more interesting. Bonus points if in your fantasy they burst onto the scene in dramatic fashion while you are bored out of your mind at work.

ASHLYNN

THE GUY AT THE END OF THE BAR WAS WATCHING ME. Given the nature of the establishment I worked for, this wasn't, in and of itself, a cause for alarm.

Sure, I was a bartender rather than a stripper at the Heart's Desire, but that was mostly because I couldn't dance for shit, and if a drunk customer grabbed *my* ass I'd knock him out flat before the bouncers could get to him. Given my heritage and anger management issues, there was every chance I'd forget to hold back and accidentally kill the poor idiot.

Elysians did not mix well in the mortal realm, but I hadn't been given a choice about coming here, and after a few years I'd realized all I could do was make the best of it.

The best of it had landed me at the Heart's Desire. It was pretty okay as strip clubs went, and they didn't mind my bad attitude. Mostly because the first night I'd gone verbally ballistic on a guy who'd told me to show him my tits—I'd been at a low point in my life and had somehow forgotten I was trying to tend bar at a strip club when I'd lost it—and after a moment of stunned silence, the guy had found the whole thing hilarious.

Then everyone else had found it hilarious, and it had spawned a round of, "What would you say if I asked you to do X." My smart mouth got a workout, I made a lot of tips, and I didn't get fired.

I still haven't shown anyone here the totality of my tits, but given that the dress code strongly encourages me to display them to prominent effect—which requires the liberal application of a pushup bra since mine are a comfortable B cup my back is very happy with—the patrons usually stare at them.

The guy at the end of the bar, who was definitely watching me when he thought I wasn't looking, had not once stared at my cleavage. He hadn't stared at any of the cleavage available for ogling, and there was a lot of it. He also hadn't ordered a drink. He was just...lurking.

It was a slow night, I was bored, and I wanted to know why the hell he kept looking at me.

I walked up and leaned over the bar, which put my breasts pretty much in his face. His gaze immediately snapped to my face, and I got my first good look at him. Or as good of a look as I could in the dimly-lit environ I called my job, and with him still having the hood of his sweatshirt pulled over his head.

I couldn't make out hair color because of the hoodie, or eye color because of the dim lighting, but I didn't think I knew him. He had a strong jaw, looked like he was maybe a couple years older than my twenty-four, and his posture told me he probably had a pretty good physique hiding underneath the hoodie.

"Something I can get you, sugar?"

I'd run a series of experiments testing out different pet names and determined that *sugar,* said in a thick, entirely fake

Texas drawl, resulted in the most positive response in terms of tips.

He shook his head.

"Look," I said, "here's the deal. You've been in here half an hour. You haven't bought a dance, thrown money at a stripper, or ordered a drink. It's a slow night. The bouncers are bored. You want to stay, order a drink." The bouncers probably couldn't care less, but this guy didn't look like he was likely to know that.

"Why do you work here?" he asked.

Great, so he was one of *those*. The what's-a-nice-girl-like-you-doing-in-a-place-like-this type.

"It pays the bills. You ordering a drink or not?"

"Sure."

I waited. Since it appeared I would wait until the proverbial end of time if he was left to his own devices, I prompted, "And that drink would be...?"

He shrugged. "What's your favorite?"

And one of those. "Let me give you some advice, pal. I've seen your type before. Maybe I remind you of the girl who lived next door when you were a kid. Maybe you have a savior complex but you don't quite want to try to reform a stripper, so the bartender looks like a safe enough bet.

"Whatever it is, I don't care. I like working here. It tips a lot better than Starbucks. I don't need to be rescued, and I don't have time to give any fucks about whatever emotional crisis you're going through. I'm not telling you my favorite drink, what I wanted to be when I grew up, and I'm not going to cry on your shoulder.

"If you don't order a drink in the next fifteen seconds, *I'll* throw you out, and I'll be far less gentle about it than the bouncers would be."

He finally looked straight at me for the first time, but the neon lights still made it impossible to make out his eye color.

The barest hint of a smile tugged at the corners of his lips. I couldn't help but notice they were good lips. Exceptionally high on the kissability scale.

Why were all the hot ones crazy?

"Then I'll have a whiskey soda." The words rolled off his lips a little strangely, like he'd never ordered a drink at a bar before, and was repeating the line like a script.

He reminded me of *me* when I'd first landed in this hellscape the mortals called home. Granted, I'd been twelve at the time, so I hadn't been ordering drinks at bars, but I hadn't known how to act. I'd been used to running wild with werewolves, tempting my luck at the outskirts of Fae territory, and trying to piss off Dragons, among other things. Once I'd landed here, it had taken me a little longer than it probably should have to stop trying to convince people those things were real.

I'd bounced from foster home to foster home, each one increasingly unimpressed with my story of being banished from my birthplace of Elysium, along with five other girls my age. Those girls were the reason it had taken me so long to shut my mouth about magic. Because I didn't know where they were. Because I'd wanted to find them, to make sure they were okay.

But I'd shut up once I'd understood precisely what could happen in the mortal world to a kid with no family, whom everyone thought was insane.

I poured the whiskey soda and thunked it down in front of the stranger, a little more violently than necessary. As a rule, I tried not to think about my childhood. The half spent here, because it had been shit, and the half before, because it had been perfect.

Perfect, until Elysium's Oracle had announced that the Darkness was waking, and only sending six girls, all twelve years old, into the mortal realm would avert disaster. It was a load of bullshit if you asked me, but of course, the Elysian Elders hadn't.

After a few years, I'd stopped trying to find my way home. Near as I could tell, there *wasn't* a way home. And once I'd gotten older, I'd had enough anger to think maybe the place didn't deserve to be called my home anymore.

My bad mood stuck with me the rest of the night, even after business picked up and the stranger left. Later, after the place closed up and I was in the locker room, peeling myself out of skintight jeans and fuck-me boots, I slipped off the lace arm sleeves I wore to cover my tattoos, and looked at the names inked into my skin.

Brialyn. Beryl. Seraphina. Haven. Leanna. Ashlynn.

The last was my own. I'd hesitated to add it, but in the end it had felt right, nestled with the others. Three names on the inside of each forearm, six in total. My sisters. Not by blood, but by circumstance.

There was a seventh name inked on my body, one I hid with makeup because it was placed over my heart. It wasn't that the club cared whether its employees had tattoos or not. It was that I didn't want to answer the inevitable questions.

I didn't bother taking the makeup off as I switched shirts, so I couldn't actually *see* the name written there, but I felt it, like a brand newly burned into my skin: *Luca.*

Most people would see the placement of that name on my body and come to the wrong conclusion, but I'd put it there for a very specific reason. Because I'd decided the person who'd served my greatest betrayal deserved a place of honor, so I would never forget what he'd done.

Dramatic, since I was unlikely to ever see him again? Perhaps. But it served its purpose.

I finished changing into my normal clothes and walked out the back of the club. My motorcycle lounged in the parking lot, a little red Honda Shadow. She'd been a work in progress when I bought her, but months of steady tips had seen her restored to her true glory. I swung my leg over the bike and brought her roaring to life. I'd barely started her up when I had the sense that I was being watched.

I surveyed the parking lot but I didn't see anyone. In all likelihood, I was just keyed up from the weird stranger and the remembrance of things best left forgotten. And if I wasn't, if it turned out to be something more than that, well, I could more than take care of myself. An unhealthily large part of me would even enjoy the excuse to take my frustration out on someone else.

I didn't live far from the Heart's Desire, but that sense of being watched followed me the entire way. When I pulled into my apartment building's parking lot I killed the engine and sat for a moment. I pretended to scroll through my phone, but really, I was listening. My hearing was better than the average human's—not as good as it was in Elysium, for coming here had muted what I truly was, but it was nothing to sneeze at. So I sat and listened, waiting for something. Anything.

A light breeze shifted the July air, hot and stifling in Phoenix, Arizona even in the dead of night. The wind carried the various refuse of mortal life across the rough asphalt—the scuttle of an abandoned plastic water bottle, the rustle of an empty chip bag. Cars flew by on the highway that ran alongside the apartment complex, a never-ending drone of traffic. They called New York the city that never sleeps, but it seemed to me that mentality had taken a foothold in the whole of the mortal realm.

The constant noise had been disorienting when I'd first come here. I didn't like it any better now, but I'd learned to block out the meaningless everyday noises so I didn't go insane, and I was eternally grateful my hearing wasn't *as* good here as it had been in Elysium. I still had to wear earplugs to sleep, though.

Right now, I didn't block anything out. I listened to everything, sifted through the sounds that didn't matter, tracking the one that would lead back to that persistent feeling of being watched. In the end, it wasn't a sound at all. It was the absence of sound, a pocket of quiet that was *too* quiet in this land of endless noise.

I tucked my phone into my pocket and swung off the bike. Instead of heading up the three flights of stairs to my apartment I walked around the unit, aiming for the little courtyard in the center that contained a sad excuse for a kid's playground, and a dog run only chihuahuas were small enough to find stimulating.

The silence, the emptiness, followed. Discreetly, at a distance, but it followed. I hadn't encountered anything here that moved like that. Nothing human, anyway. If you went far enough out to what little wild still existed in this country, you could find the predators that had that grace, that easiness, that stillness. But I wasn't in the wilderness, and while coyotes stalked through this city, coyotes didn't feel like this, and they certainly didn't follow one woman around.

I only knew one thing that moved like this, hunted like this: werewolf. But for all that the mortals had legends of them here, I'd never run across an actual werewolf outside of Elysium. It had to be something else.

But as I sped up, ducked around the playground slide and vaulted silently up to the top of it, then from there into the large non-native pine tree planted next to it, my senses insisted the same thing: *werewolf, werewolf, werewolf.*

My pursuer stepped into the soft glow of the playground lamppost, and it wasn't a werewolf. It was the damn stranger from the bar, Mr. Whiskey Soda himself.

I wasn't afraid. Part of me wished I could be, because if I

could feel fear, I might feel a little more alive. But there wasn't much that could hurt me in this world, and one run-of-the-mill stalker wasn't going to do it. I was glad he'd fixated on me instead of one of the other women at the club. They were all careful. They all took precautions. But no one should have to be constantly *expecting* to be followed and attacked.

I did, because the fight, the hunt, was in my nature. And if I couldn't go home, I could at least have a little fun and teach this asshole a lesson. I dropped silently from the tree at a trajectory that would knock him down flat. Or it would have, if he'd still been there when I landed.

He stepped aside at the last second, faster than a human could move, and I landed in a crouch on the ground instead. I rolled away and to my feet, putting distance between us, prepared for an attack that didn't come.

"Sloppy," he said. "Your toe scraped bark on the way down." I hadn't been able to hear the nuances of his voice in the bar but here, in the open night air, it was a deep, rich rumble that slid over me like molten honey.

He stood six feet away, the hood of his sweatshirt still pulled up over his head. His hands were tucked casually into his pockets, like he couldn't be bothered to take me seriously as a threat. The grace and power that hummed beneath his skin, though, the primal way he held himself that spoke of sensuality and violence, screamed the same thing my instincts had earlier: *werewolf.*

What the fuck? He couldn't be a werewolf. For one, they didn't come here. For another, I would have smelled him in the damn club. Except there were so *many* scents in a strip club it became overwhelming, and I did my best to tamp down my senses there because, honestly, I didn't *want* to smell the things that went on in that place

"Who the fuck are you?"

He canted his head at me. "You don't know, Ash?"

My pulse quickened and I told myself it didn't matter, absolutely didn't matter, that he knew my name. Every creature in Elysium knew my name. Mine, and five others. That was the joy of being prophecy-named. It didn't mean I'd met this particular werewolf, even if I had spent a great deal of my childhood running wild with the White Woods Pack.

Still, I wondered, if he pulled that stupid hood off, would his hair be winter blond?

"If I did know," I said, "I wouldn't be asking. But now, I'm thinking I don't really care. Wolves understand territory, so I'll be clear. This is mine. Get the fuck out of it."

When I was a kid, I'd dreamed someone from Elysium would come here to find me. They would defy the Elders' orders, search the mortal realm, and bring me home. That someone had always been a very specific person, in my childhood fantasies.

When I'd turned sixteen, I'd finally understood that no one was coming for me. A couple years ago, I'd realized I didn't even want them to. Because Elysium wasn't my home anymore. It had ceased being my home the moment everyone in it had tossed me out into this world alone, with no resources and no family, because a goddamn oracle had told them it was for the greater good.

The wolf in human form raised one eyebrow. "This, as in, this square of grass we're standing in, or this, as in, this shitty labyrinth of buildings?"

Son of a bitch had a smart mouth on him. "This, as in, the mortal world."

"You know, a wolf can only claim the territory he can hold. I don't think you can reasonably claim the entirety of the mortal realm."

"I can and I just fucking did. Unless you brought your whole pack with you, the only person I need to defend it from is you. And frankly, you don't look like much of a challenge."

"Why don't we find out?" he taunted.

I attacked, my body humming with joy as I embraced the entirety of my Elysian heritage and unleashed it on him. My gift was the hunt, the fight, and I missed it sorely, missed having an opponent who was an actual challenge.

And damn, he was good. We moved in tandem, dodging and striking, dancing around each other with a fluidity that made my heart sing. Most fights turned to grappling matches sooner rather than later, but though I'd intended to simply put him down, I found myself sparring more than fighting to win, because I hadn't felt this alive in years.

He was beautiful to fight, lighter on his feet than anyone with a werewolf's weight and bulk had any right to be. So many wolves counted on brute strength to win a fight but this one, this one had trained, learned to use his brain as well as his brawn, and his movements were familiar.

Oh, they were more graceful than they had been in his youth, more smooth and practiced, but they were still the same.

It's not him. Plenty of people could fight similarly, if they had the same teacher. It didn't mean anything, and I could stop fucking around and prove it.

I fell into a predictable pattern of moves, one that always left my right side open. Eventually, he went for it. When he did, I sidestepped, whipped my leg behind his and took him out at the knees. I was on him as he fell. I straddled him, pinned his legs with mine, his arms above his head.

When it came to brute strength, werewolves had more than just about anyone else in Elysium, even me. But he didn't have a werewolf's full strength in the mortal realm. And he didn't fight me. He looked, in fact, like he had me right where he wanted me.

He laughed, a deep rumble that vibrated through me in all the places we touched, and the hood fell back from his face. Blond hair, so light it was almost white. Blue eyes like ice in winter.

"Luca," I whispered.

"Hey, Ashlynn."

❧ 2 ❧

LUCA

I wasn't all that surprised when Ash hauled back and punched me. She'd always had a temper that was one spark shy of setting the world on fire. I took the hit because I deserved it. I deserved a lot worse.

I'd failed her. She'd been my best friend, and she'd been so scared when the Oracle's prophecy came out. Scared, and desperately unwilling to show it. I'd promised I wouldn't let anything happen to her. I'd tried to keep that promise. I had the scars on my wrists and ankles to prove it, but in the end it didn't matter. The result had been the same, and she had every right to be pissed.

Still, when she hauled back to hit me a second time, I caught her fist in my palm, shifted my hips, flipped, and pinned her beneath me.

"Get the fuck off me, Luca."

I grinned at her, because I couldn't help it. "Maybe I like being here."

Damn, but Ashlynn had grown up. I'd known she wouldn't be a kid anymore, that *we* weren't kids anymore, but I hadn't put any thought into what she might have grown into.

Hot as fuck just about summed it up, and fighting had always been my favorite kind of foreplay. I was desperately trying to remember that I'd come here for a reason, but suddenly all I wanted to do was bury my face in the curve of her neck, breathe in her scent, and kiss my way down to the breasts she'd all but shoved in my face in that disgusting place the mortals called a club.

"Hey, keep your goddamn werewolf sex drive to yourself," she snapped. "I'm not interested."

"That's a shame." And a lie, to some degree. She smelled like excitement and lust, and it was a heady combination. Still, just because a little rough-and-tumble got her wet didn't mean she wanted to fuck me. And I'd never had any interest in an unwilling partner.

She snorted. "Since I hardly think you came all the way from Elysium, after twelve goddamn years, to *seduce me*, let me reiterate. What the ever-loving fuck are you doing here?"

She was half wrong. The Elders had sent me here to bring her home and—well, seduce her wasn't quite the spirit of the command, but the Oracle's latest prophecy about the Six and the Darkness had involved another layer I wasn't comfortable with.

Some bullshit about each of the Six having a mate destined to stand at their side. I hadn't believed in prophecy at fifteen, when the entire island had listened to the Oracle spew his nonsense about how if the Six weren't sent from Elysium, the returning Darkness would worsen, and I didn't believe it now.

But Elysium *had* believed, and they'd sent six fucking children into a land they knew nothing about to fend for themselves, and when I'd tried to follow Ashlynn—I shook my head. Better not to relive that. By the time I'd escaped my chains, the Elders had sealed the borders of Elysium so tightly I couldn't leave the island.

And the Darkness had grown stronger anyway. Oh, it hadn't fully broken through, but its tendrils snaked through Elysium now, and the woods at night were no longer safe. When the occurrences first happened, I had thought the Elders would finally come to their senses. That they'd unlock the border and find the Six.

But then the damn Oracle had opened his mouth with a second prophecy, one no doubt fabricated to save his own hide. And my people had let their collective guilt at what they'd done be assuaged by the Oracle's assurance that only by living twelve years in the mortal realm could the Six be made strong enough to defeat the coming Darkness. They could only be found and brought back to Elysium by their destined mates, and only survive the Darkness if they accepted those mates.

The prophetic asshole had given himself so many loopholes that when Elysium inevitably fell to the Darkness and it overtook the mortal world, he had a dozen things he could point to and say, *See? X didn't happen. Not my fault.*

It hadn't escaped my notice that saying the Six could *only* be retrieved by their supposedly destined mates meant the chances of finding them were exceptionally low. The mortal realm was a much larger one than Elysium. But I hadn't cared. I'd bided my time, and two days ago, the night before the twelve years was up, I'd cornered the Oracle in his home and told him if he didn't name me as Ashlynn's mate in the announcement ceremony the next day, I'd rip his fucking throat out.

Because I had a promise to keep, and I didn't trust anyone else to bring her home. And *I* would never try to force her to fuck me, but I didn't trust some other pompous asshole hyped up on oracular nonsense about destiny and his fucking rights not to give it a go.

She'd probably kill anyone that tried, but I hadn't known

how growing up in the mortal world would affect her. I hadn't been willing to risk it.

If protecting her meant giving up any chance of settling down with a mate of my own, it would be worth it. Because I owed her. Because she was Ashlynn. And she had, in some ways, always been mine. Mine to protect.

Her deep brown eyes stared up at me, and I realized she was waiting for an answer to a question.

"I'm here to bring you home, Ash."

3

ASHLYNN

I'M HERE TO BRING YOU HOME. IF HE'D SHOWED UP AND SAID those words to me years ago, I probably would have forgiven him everything. I would have forgiven everyone everything, because I'd been so desperately homesick and miserable here.

But I wasn't a kid anymore, and I wasn't interested in forgiving anyone for what they'd done to me.

"I'm not going anywhere with you. Get off me."

"Ash—"

"Get. Off. Me."

Luca rolled back and let me up. I missed the warmth of him immediately, and I told myself it was just because I hadn't been properly laid in some time. I'd given it another go a few nights past, but while the guy had been very pretty on the outside, he'd been spectacularly bad in bed. Not to mention clingy. It'd taken me an hour to get him out of my apartment the next morning, and he still wouldn't stop texting me.

I regained my feet and stalked past Luca. He simply fell into step beside me.

"Where are you going?" he asked.

"To my *actual* home. It's a crappy apartment that costs a ridiculous amount of money, because that's what living in this world is."

I bounded up the steps and unlocked the door to my apartment, Luca right on my heels. I tried to slam the door in his face but he shoved back and blew past me inside.

"It doesn't have to be. What happened to you wasn't right, but you don't have to be alone out here anymore."

"What happened to me?" Anger was a burning flame in my gut. "What *happened* to me? You make it sound like a fucking accident, Luca. My own people threw me out like trash because *one* person told them it was sacrifice the children or else the Darkness comes. So what now? Did the Oracle open his mouth again and tell you to bring us back?"

A muscle twitched along Luca's jaw and he didn't answer.

No fucking way. "He *did*, didn't he? Well, I'm so glad that everyone's still jumping at his every command. I'm so *glad* that, now it's convenient for you, you've decided to come find out if I'm alive."

"I didn't come for you because it was convenient, Ash. I came for you because I *can* now. The Elders locked the borders down after you left. I *couldn't* follow you."

I shook my head. It didn't matter. He'd promised he wouldn't let them send me away. Even then I hadn't been naive enough to believe he could work miracles and change the whole of Elysian opinion. But I *had* believed him when he'd said that if he couldn't, he would come with me. That he wouldn't let me be alone.

So I hadn't been as scared as I should have been that day. But Luca hadn't shown, and when the Elders had shoved me through to the mortal world, I'd been completely alone. Still, I'd believed in him so much I'd stupidly thought he'd come after me. That something had held him up, but he would still come for me.

I hadn't worried about where I was, hadn't done much beyond finding shelter and scavenging for food while I waited for him to appear, certain that if I stayed in the same area, his werewolf nose would find me. But he hadn't found me, and now I knew he'd never even come to the mortal world to look.

What he'd said about the Elders locking the border didn't change anything. Because I *knew* the spell that closed Elysium off. It took weeks to enact. Weeks that he'd had to come for me and hadn't.

"Tell yourself whatever you need to if it makes you feel better," I said. "I'm done letting my life be dictated by others. Including you. Get the fuck out."

When he didn't move, I grabbed his wrist and pulled him toward the door. He came with me one step, then broke my grip. His arms closed around my waist, pulled me to him until my back was flush against his body.

"I'm sorry, Ashlynn," he whispered, his breath soft against the shell of my ear. "I missed you."

I missed you too, I thought.

Every muscle in my body purred at being wrapped in his embrace, being pressed against him. I'd always been comfortable with him, and though I'd been too young to think of him like *this* in Elysium, I'd understood a few years later that I probably would have in time, if I'd been allowed to stay.

Because Luca was *mine*. He'd always been mine, from the first time I'd laid eyes on him when I was six years old and told him I thought he'd make the perfect little Hunter's hound.

I would never forget the indignant fury that had lit those blue eyes. We'd had our first sparring match right then and there. He'd won that one, because he was older. He hadn't won so many after.

"You don't get to miss me," I said. "You let me go."

"I didn't want to. I tried not to." He nuzzled the side of my neck and breathed in—breathed in my scent, breathed in *me*. "You smell just like I remember." Against my neck, his lips curved into a smile. "Can't say you look the same though. You sure as hell grew up."

Heat flushed my chest. Stupid werewolf sex drives. Once a werewolf mated, they did so for life. *Before* a werewolf mated, they tended to give promiscuous a new name.

Luca clearly hadn't mated yet, if the way he'd wrapped himself around me was any indication. Werewolves were extremely physical. I was pretty physical myself, and every one of my hormones chose that moment to remind me I hadn't had good sex in a while, and that everything about Luca pushed my buttons.

If I didn't say something, I'd be tempted to delay the rest of this argument until I'd stripped him naked and climbed him like a jungle gym.

"Yeah, well, you grew up too," I said, making my lips form words. Ugh. Those were not the right words. The right words were, *Get the fuck out of my apartment, Luca.*

"Do you like it?" he asked.

Yes. Aloud, I said, "You're not really my type."

His arms tensed around me. "What's your type?"

I shrugged. Best to firmly put him off now. I lied my ass off. "Taller. Darker. Handsomer. Funnier. Smar—"

"I get it," he growled, and did the thing my words had been chosen to make him do: he let me go.

Wolves. So *prickly*. Especially where their pride was concerned.

I walked to the fridge, pulled out a beer and tossed it at Luca's head. He caught it on reflex. I grabbed another for myself and downed half of it before I turned back to him.

I was still having trouble believing he was here. That he wasn't a hallucination. I'd spent so much of my childhood in the mortal world being told I was crazy that it was difficult to wrap my head around the reality of him. Oh, none of the adults had said the word "crazy" to my face. No, the foster parents, social workers, and therapists had all simply tried to impress upon me that my stories about Elysium and its magical inhabitants, my belief in my own non-mortal origins, were the result of a traumatic break, likely caused by whatever had resulted in my being dumped in the desert.

And when I'd first arrived here, I hadn't had enough of my Elysian abilities left to prove what I was. I'd been a little stronger than the average kid, but that simply got attributed to the ever-present rage I had going on. Even though I'd known I wasn't crazy, that Elysium had been real, if you're told something over and over again enough times, you start to wonder if maybe everyone else is right about you.

Luca, standing here, was proof they weren't. Proof that I wasn't crazy, that I'd never been crazy, and I didn't know how to feel about him. On the one hand, I was so stupidly grateful to see him, to see anyone from Elysium, that I desperately wanted him to stay. I wanted him to touch me again, because when he touched me I was certain he was real. On the other hand, I was so hurt and mad at him that I wanted to punch him again.

Ask him, I thought. *Ask him to explain.* But what could he say that would matter? It wouldn't change what had happened. And I didn't want to be disappointed in the answer.

I drained the rest of the beer. "If you really *are* sorry, you owe me. I want you to take me to the others."

"The others?"

As if he didn't know.

"The rest of the Six." I thrust my arms out, baring their inked names. I'd looked for them, but I'd never found a trace of them. Not that I'd really expected to.

I had always been warned, as a child, not to swim out to the border that ran around the island of Elysium. My father had told me that it was mercurial, and even if two people were to exit the border at the same place, they might arrive in two entirely different places in the mortal realm. So if I were to go through by accident, it would be difficult for another Elysian to come through and find me. Which was why, when I'd come through to the mortal world, I'd landed in a desert in the-middle-of-nowhere Arizona, and hadn't found a trace of the other girls that had been sent through.

I hadn't been able to find Elysium itself because the Elders had ripped out my Heartstone, the gem all Elysians are born with. It rests over the heart, a flat stone that grows seamlessly in with the skin. It channels the majority of our abilities, and it is the thing that makes Elysium recognize us as belonging to the island.

When the Elders tore mine from my chest, Elysium no longer recognized me. Without my own Heartstone, or having direct physical contact with someone still possessed of theirs, I would never find Elysium on my own.

Which begged the question, had the Elders destroyed my Heartstone? And if they hadn't, had Luca brought it with him? I focused on him, tried to sense my Heartstone, but I couldn't. I couldn't even sense *his*, and I didn't know if that was because the glamour that clearly hid it from mortal sight hid it from me as well, or if it was something...else.

"I don't know where the others are, Ash."

"The Elders sent you to find us all and you don't know where they are?"

"They didn't send me to find all of the Six. Only you."

"I have a difficult time believing that. You found me. You must be able to do the same for them."

"The Elders found you. *They* sent me to the right place."

I shook my head. "I don't—"

He cut me off. "In case you've forgotten, you weren't the only person I lost that day. They took my sister, too." He took my arm, running his finger over one of the names inked there. *Leanna.* "Do you honestly believe I'd stand here and lie to you about being able to find the others when she's out here somewhere?"

Leanna. She and I had not been close. She and Luca had not been particularly close. But he had always been fiercely protective of her. If he could find the others, he *would* find her.

"They'll be found and brought back. All of them. Just not by me."

"And you're just okay with that? With trusting your *sister's* life to someone else?" And if he could only come for one of us, why had he come for me and not her?

"I didn't have a choice. The only choice I had was to come for you, or not at all. So yes, I have to trust my sister's life to someone else. So if you want to see her, to see all of them, you need to come back with me."

I shook my head. "Elysium turned its back on me. *You* turned your back on me. Why the hell would I go with you?"

"The Darkness is spreading, Ash. People are dying."

I laughed—not at the people dying part, but at the Darkness. I laughed so hard I doubled over and it took me a minute to fight through breathless tears enough to speak.

"So you're telling me the Oracle said to send us away to *stop* the Darkness and it didn't work, so now he's telling you to bring us *back* to stop the Darkness?"

Luca's jaw clenched.

"We have a term here in this world. It's called a con artist. See, a con artist fabricates a lie to get something they want— money, notoriety, whatever—and then, when people figure out it was all a bunch of bullshit and things start to go sideways, the con artist piles more lies on top of the original lie in order to placate people. And for that to work, whatever he's selling has to be good enough that people *want* to believe what he's saying is true."

Luca finally unhinged his jaw. "I'm not an idiot, Ash. I know it's all bullshit."

I blinked. "Then why the hell would you jump at the Elders' bidding to come bring me back?"

"Because *I* want you back. Because it may be bullshit, but the Darkness *is* spreading, and we're losing to it. And I think that if the Six came back we could fight it. Not because of some damn prophecy but because you all were the best of us."

Legend claimed that Elysium's sole purpose was to guard the mortal world against the Darkness that would otherwise consume it. Elysium itself was a prison, the six-pointed star at the island's center the gate that held that prison closed. Some even said that Elysium was built to change the Darkness. That our powers, our Heartstones, came from the purification of the Darkness beneath our lands.

Whatever the reality was, the Darkness started spreading through Elysium the year I was born. Little cracks in the six-pointed star. Stories about Dark things lurking in the forest shadows. Year after year, it got a little bit worse, and year after year, the fear grew. Until the Oracle proclaimed the Darkness could be stopped. All they had to do was banish the six magically-strongest individuals born the same year as the gate's sickness, one for each point on the star.

"I've never fought the Darkness, Luca. And I may have survived having my Heartstone ripped out, but I'm a fraction of myself without it."

I hadn't known if any of my abilities would come back after that mutilation. It had taken long, agonizing years for them to return at all, and they had grown steadily, if slowly, but I still wasn't what I would have been in Elysium. What I would be with my Heartstone.

"They still have it. They'll give it back if you come home."

The desire to have my Heartstone back was so strong, I almost said yes. What would it be like to be whole again? To have my true power back? To be *me* again?

"And what's the price?" I bit off. "What are the Elders going to demand in exchange for its return?" I wasn't so naive as to think they would hand it over for nothing. The Elders—all of Elysium, really—had a deep mistrust and disdain for the mortal realm. Any Elysian who visited it often was considered an oddity. I had grown up here. What would they think of me?

"Just come back," Luca growled.

Ah. So whatever it was, I *really* wouldn't like it.

"You never used to dance around a subject so much."

He *still* didn't say anything.

"You know, of everyone I used to know, I never thought *you'd* turn into the Elders' little bitch. What? Was being pack prince not enough for you? You needed the whole goddamn island to fall at your feet?"

His hands balled into fists, and veins popped out along his forearms. The wolf showed in the dark sheen that rolled over his eyes.

"Think whatever you want, Ash. You're going to anyway. And you obviously don't care about anyone but yourself. But the truth is, I didn't come here to negotiate. I didn't come here to give you a choice. You can come back to Elysium with me, or I can drag you back. Take the night. Think it over."

I wanted to tell him he could *try* to drag me back, but retorts never landed quite the same when directed at a wolf, and he shifted too fast for me to reply a human. Power rent the air around him, bones cracked, and Luca was gone. The wolf that stood in his place was the same color I remembered, brilliant white fur that ended in silver tips, but the resemblance to the pup I'd known ended there.

This wolf's head was at the same height as my shoulders, his chest as broad as a draft horse's and his paws... As a kid, I hadn't understood the jokes about the size of a werewolf's paws indicating the size of certain other parts of their anatomy. But now, the adult me was curious, despite my monumental present anger, to know if that rumor was true.

Darkness, if I was really thinking about *that* right now, I needed to get laid even more badly than I'd thought. Thank Elysium's six-pointed star Luca couldn't read my thoughts. Werewolves could communicate mentally with other weres in wolf form, but the only way a human could mentally communicate with a wolf was if they declared a mating bond.

And there was no way in mortal hell or Elysian Darkness I was ever entering into a mating bond with Luca Ferrar. Not now that he'd turned out to be a colossal asshole as well as the friend who'd abandoned me.

He padded over to the front door, dropped down in front of it, and laid his head on his paws.

"Don't expect breakfast in the morning. I'm all out dog food." It'd be nice if I could storm into my bedroom and forcefully slam the door. Unfortunately, I lived in a studio apartment, so I had to settle for dropping onto my bed and turning my back to him.

I wasn't tired, and even if I had been, the idea of falling asleep while his wolf lounged ten feet away was a difficult one to get on board with. I closed my eyes anyway, and though I tried hard not to, I found his presence a comfort.

I'd always hated sleeping alone, and as a child, I rarely had. When I'd grown too old to slip into my parents' bed with made up claims about nightmares, I'd found Luca. And so long as he remained in wolf form, the adults hadn't minded our constant sleepovers. We'd grown up half in each others' worlds, me trying to run with the wolves, and him trying to control his lupine nature at an age too young for most wolves to manage spending time outside their pack.

And here, though I'd tried hard not to admit it, every time I brought a stranger home, it wasn't the sex I wanted. I mean, sure, I *wanted* sex. But what I was looking for was Luca, and that steady presence I'd lost.

I listened for his breaths, counted each one in and out, in and out, until mine fell in rhythm with his, and I finally slept.

❧ 4 ❧

LUCA

I squeezed my eyes shut, buried my nose between my paws, and did my best to look dead asleep. Barely an hour with her and I'd already made a mess of things.

Tell her she's a self-centered bitch, Luca, that'll get her to come home.

I snorted into my paws and forgot too late that I was pretending to be asleep. Which was really just the icing on the cake, that my people skills were now so bad I'd gone wolf and played dead just to get out of a damn conversation.

I'd known she wouldn't understand why I hadn't come for her before now. I hated myself for not finding a way to go with her all those years ago. But she hadn't even *tried* to let me explain. Not that I could. Not without telling her those other little details about why the Elders had let me come for her now, details that would drive her away quicker than her simply thinking I was a dick.

And though it might have been harsh, I'd told her the truth: I *would* drag her back to Elysium if I had to. The Darkness had only grown worse in the years since her banishment. The woods were barely even safe for the wolves at night. The things that slunk and slithered through the trees grew bolder month by month, and I wondered when they would no longer keep to the woods, to the shadows, at all.

Worse, though, was the sickness. The woods could be avoided. The shadows could be watched. But we couldn't fight against a sickness we didn't understand the origins of. It claimed individuals with no causal connection we could find, and it was Darkness born, if the way the veins beneath the skin turned black was any indication. Some people got better, once the Darksickness claimed them. Most didn't.

The Elders claimed they couldn't fight it. Worse, they weren't even trying. The pack patrolled the forests, and they fought the Darkness when it showed its face, but they wouldn't take the fight *to* the Darkness. No one would.

It infuriated me. Meeting after meeting, the leaders of Elysium's various factions said the same thing without fail: We must hold the line and wait. Wait for the Six to return. Wait for the prophecy to be fulfilled.

All around them their people died while they twiddled their thumbs and claimed there was nothing to be done about it. Waited, instead, for six women with no reason to do so to come back and save Elysium from a mess it had gotten itself into.

Sometimes, on the darker nights, I wondered if *that* was why the Darkness came for us. If it wasn't part of a prophecy, but simply a test. A test, to see what people would do if faced with a terrible threat, and told they could defeat it by making a choice. Elysium had made the wrong choice, and no small part of me thought that if we'd refused the Oracle's demands, if we'd never sent the Six away, maybe we wouldn't be in this mess now. Maybe the Darkness would have slunk back into its prison.

So I couldn't feel good about dragging Ash home. But I thought, if I could get her there, make her remember the good parts, that she wouldn't want to watch it burn. That she would want to fight. She'd *always* wanted to fight. And where Elysium wouldn't listen to me, the exiled, scarred prince who'd gone against his pack, gone against the Elders, they would listen to her. Because she was prophecy-named, and the fools thought that meant something.

I had to convince her. If I convinced her, she could convince the other five. And if the totality of the Six told the Elders to get off their asses and fight, surely *then* they would be out of excuses not to.

❧ *5* ❧

LUCA

I WOKE BECAUSE ONE OF THE SMALL BLACK BOXES THE mortals called cell phones wouldn't stop clanging an obnoxious noise into the room.

Ashlynn had merely grunted, flung it across the room, and gone back to sleep. Its rough landing against the wall had done nothing to deter its noise-making capabilities. I padded over to the offensive object, picked it up in my mouth and trotted across the room to drop it on her face. It was the wolf slobber, I think, that finally jolted her awake.

She jabbed her thumb at the cell phone, which mercifully stopped screeching, and rolled to sit up. Her hair was a glorious, disheveled mess and her face was flush with irritation. She wiped her palm across her cheek and glared at me.

"Your breath stinks."

I gave her a large, wolf grin.

"If that was supposed to be scary, you need to work on your game." She shoved the covers off and stood. When she moved, I moved with her. Ashlynn was *fast*. I wasn't going to risk her breaking for the door. Not that I thought she'd get very far—even her infernal transportation machine was no match for werewolf speed—but the chase, while fun, would delay things.

She rolled her eyes and walked to the small door that led to the bathroom. I didn't have any intention of following her inside, but when she went to block me, I made a show of trying to just for fun. She hip-checked me and placed herself in the doorway facing me.

"You don't need to watch me piss, Luca."

On that, we both agreed. Wonder of wonders, we had common ground after all.

She slammed the door in my face. It had barely closed when someone knocked on her front door. Since I didn't hear the sounds of her frantically finishing her business to go open it, I assumed she didn't care. Whoever it was knocked again, more insistently this time, more...concerned.

I padded over to the door and sniffed. Human. Male. Did Ashlynn have a lover? It shouldn't matter if she did, and yet the possibility rankled for some reason.

I growled, a low, warning rumble, and barked like one of the mortal dogs that seemed a fixture of half the households in this realm.

"Ash?" The man called.

I didn't like her name on his tongue.

"Are you okay in there?"

"Now you've done it," Ashlynn muttered, far too soft for the human to pick up, but easy enough for werewolf ears.

She came out of the bathroom. Her earlier irritation had morphed into a full-on glare, which she leveled at me and mouthed, "Get in the fucking bathroom."

Since I was forbidden from intentionally showing a mortal my wolf form, I got in the fucking bathroom. I heard her open the door.

"What do you want, Mark?"

A hesitant pause ensued before he said, "It's Max. Did you

get a dog?"

No, I thought, *she's started growling and barking at the door herself.*

"I didn't take up growling as a side hobby."

Ha.

"Can I meet him? Her?"

"No," she said, and her next words were clearly all for me. "Prince Snowflake is in training. He's practically feral. No manners to speak of, no endearing personality traits, he drools, and he's ugly."

"Uh, okay."

"What do you want, Mark?" she repeated.

"Max," he corrected again. "I wanted to check on you. After the other night."

I could hear the damn grin in his voice and I was very, very tempted to disobey rules about behavior in the mortal world and go rip his throat out. I hadn't *smelled* a male on her sheets, but then, they had also smelled freshly laundered.

Ashlynn did not respond to Max's statement. Her non-response had a weight to it that filled the entire apartment, and I knew precisely the look she was giving him right now. It was her, you're-taking-liberties-you-don't-have-a-right-to-and-you're-an-idiot look.

Max clearly didn't get it. "You weren't answering your phone. I wanted to make sure you were all right."

"Mark," she said pointedly, and he didn't interrupt to correct her this time, "when someone doesn't answer their phone, it usually means they don't want to talk to you. I was very clear about the one-night nature of our involvement."

"Women say that, but they don't actually mean it."

I officially hated this idiot.

"I think they do. I know I did."

"Is there someone else?"

Well, now that he mentioned it...

ASHLYNN

WHY WAS IT THAT MEN THOUGHT IF YOU DIDN'T WANT them, it had to be because another man was involved?

Unfortunately, idiot men seemed to come in pairs, because I felt power whisper through my apartment as Luca shifted, and a second later the bathroom door opened. I didn't turn to acknowledge Luca for two reasons. One, I was pissed enough that if I made eye contact we'd probably fight again. Two, he was guaranteed to be naked.

If a wolf didn't shuck their clothing before a shift, magic devoured it, and Luca had not stripped last night. What exactly did he think a naked man was going to add to this situation?

That became clear when Max's eyes widened as Luca wrapped his arms around my waist. But the asshole didn't stop there, oh, no. He dropped an affectionate kiss on my cheek, looked at Max and said, "Sweetheart, who's this?"

"Who the fuck are you?" Max demanded.

Wonderful. Now that another man had shown up, apparently I was to be relegated to the sidelines of the conversation, despite literally being stuck in the middle of it by the iron bands of Luca's arms.

I could get out of them, but it'd involve a lot of work, and if I fought a naked Luca, I wasn't convinced I wouldn't end up shagging him.

"Old friend," Luca said. He nuzzled the side of my neck—just like a territorial werewolf—and it did tingly things to my insides.

Max seemed to remember I existed. "Do all of your old friends hang out naked in your house?"

I shrugged. "Sure, if they feel like it. Go home, Mark. Don't call again." I shut the door in his face, and mercy of all mercies, he shuffled off a few seconds later. I was relatively certain I would be treated to a number of angry texts he had absolutely no right to send, but then, the block-a-number feature and I were old friends.

"You actually slept with that asshole?" Luca asked.

"Pickings are slim in the mortal world. And he was pretty. How was I supposed to know he'd be terrible in bed?"

"Pretty, huh?" Luca rumbled, and the smugness in it made me certain I'd unwittingly committed a tactical error. "I thought you said I wasn't your type."

Shit. I'd said Max was pretty. Blond haired, blue-eyed Max. When backed into a corner, I'd always found it best to counter with an attack.

"I didn't need *your* help with my personal life."

Luca snorted. "Sounded like you did. The guy was starstruck. I'm surprised he didn't propose a mating bond on the spot. *You* may not have had a good time last night, but it sounded like he did."

"Yeah, well, I'm exceptional in bed. Unfortunately, I'm not sure he knows female orgasms exist, much less how to make one happen."

Luca's hands flattened on my stomach and drifted lower, perilously close to territory he had not been invited into.

He whispered in my ear, his voice low and full of promise. "I know female orgasms exist. And I definitely know how to make one happen. Should I demonstrate?"

Mmm, yes, please. "No," I snapped. "How long have you been gone from Elysium? You can't be that hard up for sex already."

"Sexually deprived? No. Hard up? Guilty."

Okay, that was enough of *that*. I broke out of the too-enjoyable circle of his arms and turned to face him. Which was a mistake because he was, as I'd suspected, bare-ass naked. The man couldn't have grabbed a damn towel from the bathroom before flaunting himself out here?

And with a body like that, all he had to do to flaunt it was exist. His shoulders were strong and broad, flowing into strong pectorals and down to the waterfall of washboard abs and—

Do not look lower, I commanded myself.

I looked lower. He was indeed hard up. Being a werewolf, he had absolutely zero shame about the fact his cock was standing at attention. And that saying about the size of a werewolf's paws? Definitely true. Luca was *hung*. I was fairly certain that if I wrapped my fist around him, my fingers wouldn't touch, and if I straddled him, I could sink down onto him for days.

"See something you like, sweetheart?"

Yes, I will take one of those, please and thank you.

"Just verifying that the reason your intellectual capacity is so small is because all of your blood lives in the southern half of your body."

"You mean my brain's so small because my other head is so large?" he asked innocently.

"You have an overinflated opinion of your own self-worth.

You may have a great cock, but that doesn't mean you know what to do with it."

Well, that was the worst possible thing I could have said. Comparing what the young me knew about werewolves to what the adult me knew about sex, I was pretty sure that if there was a *Seducing a Werewolf 101* pamphlet, step one would be to compliment his physical assets and step two would be to challenge his ability to use them.

"Oh, I definitely do. Of course, if you'd like a demonstration of my ability to satisfy, I'm more than happy to get on my knees for you first."

Now all the blood in *my* body rushed south. I couldn't remember the last time a man had gone down on me. Not that a lot of them weren't willing, but I wasn't comfortable letting just anyone down there, and I didn't form a lot of long-term sexual partnerships. Read, pretty much none.

Luca's eyes hazed over with lust, and I knew he must be scenting mine. He stalked toward me, slowly, a predator's approach, and stopped just shy of me. I couldn't stop my gaze from roving over his body again.

"You can touch, if you like," he rumbled.

I shouldn't. I definitely shouldn't. But they didn't make abs like these in the mortal world. Not off the big screen, or away from gym-junkies anyway. I splayed my hand across his stomach, traced my fingers over the ridged muscles. His eyes closed halfway and his cock twitched.

I was just thinking that maybe I *would* take him for a ride before I sent him packing back to Elysium when I saw the scars on his wrists. I could only blame the impressiveness of his physique for the fact I hadn't noticed them before.

I cursed and pulled his hand to me, examining the inch-wide band that encircled his wrist. Thick and raised, only one thing could leave a mark like that on a werewolf. Silver.

"Who did this to you?" I demanded. Silver use against

werewolves was outlawed in Elysium, unless a wolf had gone feral and the Elders sanctioned its use to put them down. Even then, they only sanctioned it if the pack alpha refused to take care of the problem themselves.

"It doesn't matter."

"The hell it doesn't, this is barbaric." Yes, silver burned a werewolf. Yes, they were slower to heal from it. But for silver to leave an actual scar required repeated exposure. For it to leave one like this would require days, *weeks* of contact.

Contact that would cause agony. Cuffs. The marks looked like cuffs. I looked down and saw the same scars around his ankles. Chained. Luca had been chained in silver.

But who in Elysium would be suicidal enough to chain the pack's prince?

"I preferred the conversation we were having before. I also preferred where you were touching me before."

I dropped his hand. I didn't have any right to push him if he didn't want to talk about it, and I told myself I didn't care, anyway.

"I'm not going to fuck you, Luca." I sounded much more certain about that fact than I felt, and my hormones gave a resounding wail of disapproval.

"That's a shame, sweetheart."

"You can drop the pet name, too."

"You started it. Prince Snowflake?" He raised an eyebrow.

"Because of your fur and your attitude. You're such a special, fragile little snowflake," I said with saccharine sweetness. "So be a good pup, and stay."

"Where are you going?"

"To take a shower." I was uncomfortably wet and something had to be done about it that didn't involve Luca. I closed the distance between us, put my hands on his shoulders and pushed onto my toes to whisper in his ear. "And

Luca? Know that everything you hear when I'm in there—that will never be for you."

I disappeared into the bathroom and turned the water so hot it was painful. I put my hand between my legs and moaned. Darkness, I couldn't remember the last time I'd been this wet. Had I *ever* been this wet? I turned the water from the showerhead to jets, let it pound my nipples while I built my orgasm. I did it slowly, and I did it loudly, and contrary to what I'd told Luca, it was absolutely all for him.

When I came, it was so loud my neighbors two doors over probably heard it, and it was all I could do not to scream Luca's name.

❧ 7 ☙

LUCA

IF I THOUGHT I'D BEEN HARD BEFORE, I WAS PAINFULLY erect when Ash started fucking herself in the shower. I hadn't thought she'd actually do it, but she wasn't being subtle, and she wasn't faking it. I could smell her arousal through the water and the closed door, hear her heart rate and her breathing speed up.

There was nothing for it. I was already naked. I took my cock in my fist and stroked it.

If someone had told me twenty-four hours ago I'd be jacking off in Ash's apartment while she did the same thing fifteen feet away, I'd have told them they were Darksick.

But her breaths were getting shorter, her moans were getting louder, and I was three-quarters there just listening to her. I fisted myself harder, faster, in time with the rhythm she set, and when she came with a shuddering scream, my balls drew tight and I spilled myself all over her kitchen floor.

I took a moment to recover and considered that I'd just come harder than I could ever remember, and I hadn't even been physically touching a woman. If Ash's world had been similarly rocked, it didn't show, as normal shower sounds commenced and she started singing, loudly and with a distinct twang, a tune about someone having to set a bad example.

I found a towel in one of the kitchen drawers and cleaned up the mess I'd made. Then I retrieved the bag of spare clothes I'd left on her balcony yesterday afternoon. I'd tracked her scent to her apartment first, only to find her gone, and criss-crossed trails all over this city before I'd finally found her at the club.

I pulled a shirt on right as she stepped out of the bathroom, wrapped in a towel that barely covered the important bits. Her legs were long and muscled, and thank Elysium I had jeans on so my cock's attempt to be interested again didn't show.

She noticed me noticing her, flashed me a wicked smile and said, "Was it as good for you as it was for me?"

"I don't know. How good was it for you? Maybe we should compare notes."

"I would, but I have places to be." She went to the closet and tossed a few things onto the bed.

"The only place you need to be going is home."

She made a *tsking* noise in the back of her throat, like she was embarrassingly disappointed in me. "I told you. I'm not going back."

"And I told you—" I cut off when she casually whipped the towel off, revealing every gloriously naked inch of her. The skin over her heart looked a slightly different shade, and I jumped at the chance to focus on anything other than how much I wanted to to walk over and take her naked body in my hands.

I smelled the chemical tang of makeup, and wondered if she was covering the scar where her Heartstone had been. Such a thing had made sense at the club she worked at, but I wasn't sure why she'd bothered today, when the shirt she'd flung out of the closet had a neckline that would cover her chest.

She picked up a pair of extremely lacy green underwear and stepped into them, then reached for the matching bra. I was relatively certain that watching a woman put lingerie *on* was not supposed to be erotic. It was the taking it off part a person was meant to enjoy. My fingers itched to go do just that, so I clasped them behind my back.

She bent over to retrieve her jeans and looked up at me through her lashes. She hadn't *needed* to fold at precisely that angle, displaying her ass and her breasts, to pick up the damn jeans.

"You were saying?" she said.

What *had* I been saying? "I have no idea. Are you having fun torturing me?"

"Of course. Besides, to use your juvenile words, you started it. I'd have given you the benefit of the doubt about your nudity in front of Max, but I see you've found clothing just fine."

"You'll thank me when Bad in Bed doesn't show up anymore."

She let out an irritated huff. "You know, Luca, he wasn't the first guy I've slept with who didn't want to take *no* for an answer the second time around. This may shock you, but I managed to get rid of the others without your help."

I didn't respond to that, because I was relatively certain there wasn't a good answer. And if I was being honest, getting involved in her argument with Max had had absolutely nothing to do with her, and everything to do with what I wanted. What I wanted was rapidly narrowing down to one thing, one person: Ash.

She pulled the rest of her clothes on, and I wasn't sure if I was relieved or disappointed at the sudden dearth of bare skin. She grabbed a set of keys, opened the door, and held her hand to usher me out.

"Well, Luca, I'd say it's been fun catching up, but—"

"We haven't caught up. You haven't asked me anything about what's happening in Elysium."

"Because I don't care. Elysium's problems stopped being my problems the moment you lot tossed me to the curb like a garbage bag."

"Elysium's problems *will* be yours if the Darkness keeps growing."

She ignored that and pointed out the door again. "I'm leaving. I don't want you here while I'm gone."

I walked out, but stayed close enough to wedge the door if her actual intention was to stay inside and lock me out. But she stepped out after me and locked the door behind her.

"You must be curious about *something*."

We walked several paces in silence before she said, "The scars. How did you get them?"

Phantom pain encircled my wrists and ankles, a reminder I didn't want. "I'm not talking about that."

She laughed. "And here I thought you wanted to catch up. Or is that you only want to talk about the things you think will make me go back?"

I tried a different tactic. "You haven't even asked about your father."

"Gosh, my father. Would that be the same man who, when I begged him not to send me away, slapped me so hard my teeth rattled and told me that true citizens of Elysium didn't question the Elders? That I should be honored to do what they said? To accept my fate if it meant Elysium would be cleansed? *That* father? You know," she snapped her fingers, "I think I don't care about him either."

We reached the infernal machine the mortals called a

motorcycle, and she swung her leg over it. A twist of the keys had the engine roaring.

"Go home, Luca," she told me. "There's nothing you can say that will convince me to come with you. And I'd *love* to see you try and make me."

Unfortunately, I was beginning to think she was right.

She rode off and left me standing in the cloud of absolutely noxious fumes the machine emitted. The mortal world was, truly, a disgusting place.

I blocked out the vehicle fumes as best I could and zeroed in on the scent of her. Based on the direction she'd turned out of the parking lot, she wasn't going back to the club from last night. I cursed the rules that kept me from shifting to wolf and set off after her, resigned to a long walk.

8
ASHLYNN

I WALKED INTO MY SECOND JOB AT EXTREME CAFFEINE, AN establishment which was anything but extreme, and tried to leave the sudden resurgence of my past behind. Sonoma and Kurt had pulled the obnoxiously early opening shifts, and now that I was here Sonoma jumped up and down excitedly and squealed, "I'm taking first lunch."

Since that was what she did every Saturday when I came in, neither Kurt nor I responded to this announcement. Neither of us knew why she bothered to declare herself on break, since she never left the employee area. No, every Saturday, without fail, she settled herself on top of the ice maker with a chocolate chip cookie and the never-ending triple-the-syrup white chocolate mocha that was permanently affixed to her hand.

Sonoma was a sugar and caffeine ingesting machine, and I had no idea how she did it.

"Okay," she said brightly, "I was saving this story for when you got here. So, you know how last week I told you Tori hooked up with Jake, *my* Jake and—"

"I thought you were dating Tanner," Kurt interrupted.

"I am. Also dating Jake. Keep up. Anyway—"

I listened to Kurt and Sonoma dissect the soap-opera worthy events of her life and idly wondered how *one* dorm could possibly contain that much drama.

I'd never gone to college. I hadn't had the money and, realistically, loans weren't worth it given how my mortal transcripts attested to my terrible suitability as a classroom student. Still, mortal culture feeds high school students a bunch of bullshit about how college is the land of hopes and dreams, and becoming one's true self, and endless other bullshit about how anything is possible.

I hadn't had any friends in high school. When I'd first gotten here, I'd been considered too crazy to befriend, and later, when I was older, too angry. By the time I realized I was completely alone—and likely to stay that way, given how poorly my search for the five other Elysians had gone—I hadn't known how to connect with anyone anymore.

So even though I'd known I would never attend college, I'd held this thought that maybe things would have been different—maybe *I* would have been different—if I had. That idiotic notion had burst into glorious flames a few months ago when Sonoma had invited me to one of the many parties she attended. Sonoma was one of those rare creatures who liked everyone until given a reason not to, and while she and I were never going to be besties, it had been nice of her to include me.

So I'd gone to the party. By that point in my life I'd consumed enough television shows to be certain that even if everything went horribly awry, it would do it in the best possible way. I would meet someone, finally find my place in the mortal world with my true love and realize my life's dream was to open a bakery or something, and whatever hot piece of man candy I ended up with at said party would conveniently have an aging relative just dying to hand over her bakery to a worthy successor.

It hadn't quite worked out that way.

I had agonized over what to wear for so long that by the time I showed up, everyone was wasted. Sonoma had been nowhere to be found, and without that one anchor in society I hadn't known what to do with myself. I'd wandered around and taken the obligatory Jello shot before some drunk guy hailed me over to the beer pong table.

I'd thought beer pong would at least be fun, but beating drunk guys was all too easy. Especially with my aim. Plus, it turned out the guy had only invited me over because he wanted to feel me up. After telling him no for the third time, after which he put his hand down my shirt anyway, I hammered a punch to his face that knocked him out cold.

His friends threw me out. Literally. It took five of them and they only managed it because I didn't fight them very hard. They also threw a Solo cup full of beer on me for good measure.

I'd come to the conclusion that partying and socializing were just never going to be for me. When I'd seen Sonoma the next day, I'd pretended I'd been unable to make it to the party and dodged all future invitations. But when her and Kurt got to talking like this, I couldn't help but be a little wistful about it. Not because I wanted that exact life, but because I wanted *a* life.

I told myself to get over it and made myself a hot americano with too many espresso shots. I'd just dumped the last one in when Sonoma straightened like a werewolf who'd scented prey, her gaze riveted on the front door.

"Oh. My. God. Hot alert. So, *so* hot alert."

I didn't bother looking. Sonoma's taste in men tended

toward would-be rock stars and stoner philosophers. Neither of which did much for me.

Kurt let out a low whistle. "For once, you and I agree. That is...delicious."

I frowned—Kurt and Sonoma *never* agreed on men—and looked to see what mythical being could manage to push both of their buttons.

Luca walked in, and from the self-satisfied grin on his face, I knew he'd heard every word of Kurt and Sonoma's exchange.

"Oh my God. How's my hair?" Sonoma asked.

"How's *my* hair?" Kurt countered.

"Neither of you need to waste time worrying about it," I muttered. "The guy's a prick."

"You *know* him?" Sonoma squeaked, and mercifully didn't have time to say anything else because Luca had reached the counter. I walked up to the register to take his order, even though the register was technically Kurt's post.

Luca unleashed a dazzling smile that had Sonoma sighing dreamily behind me.

"Ash."

"Luca." Well, wasn't this a riveting conversation? We could just say each other's names back and forth for hours until one of us expired from exhaustion.

"I thought you worked at the club."

"Poor people have multiple jobs." And the club only let me work two nights a week because, as the manager put it, "It takes a special clientele to appreciate your attitude." That special clientele knew which nights of the week they could find me at the Heart's Desire.

"You aren't poor."

"My bank account begs to differ."

"If you would just come home, money wouldn't be a problem."

A bubbling slurp behind me indicated Sonoma had hit the bottom of the liquid sugar that masqueraded as her coffee. When she did not immediately leap down to refill it, I didn't know if I should be flattered or irritated that my personal issues with Luca were so captivating she would forgo an instant refill in favor of open eavesdropping.

"Are you going to order something or not? This is a business, not a charity."

His gaze scanned the chalkboard menu on the wall behind me, as if trying to make a decision. I gave him a smile sweeter than one of Sonoma's lattes.

"Forget how to read?" It wouldn't be that he'd forgotten. It would just be that he couldn't. The magic that powered the border of Elysium was not entirely unkind—when it spit you out into the mortal realm, it made sure you could speak the predominant language of the land it dumped you into. That grace did not extend to the written language. Probably because, if Elysian lore could be believed, Elysium's border predated the development of written language.

Being a freak twelve-year-old babbling about unicorns and people with wings had been bad enough. Being one who couldn't read had opened me up to an entirely new level of derision.

"Just wondering what you recommend," Luca said finally.

"Nothing. I feel like a man should make up his own mind about what he wants."

"I don't," Sonoma said, a little breathlessly. More than a little.

Luca leaned around me and gave her a charming, wolfish smile. "Do *you* want to recommend something for me, then?"

"Do I ever." She bounced off the ice-maker. "You're going to *love* this."

I could pretty much promise he would not. Luca had never been terribly fond of sweets, so unless his tastes had changed dramatically, whatever Sonoma made him was almost guaranteed to make him nauseous. I overcharged him and took his money, wondering where he'd even gotten mortal currency.

Sonoma returned with his beverage and a bounce in her step. She handed him the cup with a pretty smile. Sonoma was, in general, pretty. A fact that never bothered me before today.

At her encouraging look, Luca lifted the cup to his mouth and took a drink. His eyes hit a particular shade of blue that conveyed pure horror to anyone who understood him.

"What do you think?" Sonoma asked earnestly.

"Yes," I prompted, "what do you think, Luca?"

"Intriguing," he managed.

"*So* glad you like it," Sonoma said.

"Indeed. Why don't you take your drink and go be *intrigued* elsewhere."

"Or stay here," Sonoma said. I glared at her.

"Here is fine," Kurt agreed. I glared at him too.

"Here is not fine. Leave, Luca, and by all means, let the door hit you on your ass on the way out."

"Good to know you're still as charming as I remember."

I smiled and leaned across the counter. "Go home. You're starting to act a bit like an abandoned dog, following someone around in the hopes they'll take pity on you and throw you a bone. I'm all out of pity, and I've never been fond of mutts."

Luca only raised an eyebrow. Damn it, he *used* to be a lot easier to offend than this. I couldn't help but wonder what had caused the change, if it had anything to do with the scars on his wrists.

He grinned at me. "You know what they say about mutts." He leaned in and whispered, "We have more fun."

I flicked him on the nose. "Bad dog."

"Does the *bad dog* want to move so the rest of us can have coffee?" an irritated voice behind Luca said.

It wasn't that I hadn't noticed the couple behind Luca walk in—my Hunter's instincts meant I couldn't *help* but notice them—it was just that I'd been more interested in getting the last word in with Luca. I was shit at customer service. Always had been.

I made a shooing motion at Luca, who thankfully sauntered—yes, *sauntered,* the prick—off, and made absolutely no attempt to apologize to the two waiting customers.

"What do you want?" I snapped.

Kurt muttered something about the tips going to hell and hip-checked me out of the way.

"Don't mind her," he said, "she's not fit for public consumption before her third cup of coffee. We usually hide her in the back."

Thirty seconds of Kurt being Kurt and they'd forgotten all about their unpleasant interaction with me. I figured the only reason I'd managed to keep this job for over a year was because no one experienced in the industry bothered applying. The coffee shop was terribly located and therefore attracted only the desperate customer.

Once the customers left, Sonoma tried and failed to observe Luca unobtrusively. He sat at a table, flipping through one of the magazines that seemed to just collect in coffee shops, his face a study in consternation.

Mortal magazines would do that to an Elysian. Even if they couldn't read what they said.

"He's still here," Sonoma whispered conspiratorially.

"Unfortunately," I said, and watched Luca's lips twitch.

"Details," Sonoma demanded.

I could refuse, which would only encourage her to pester me, or I could give her what she wanted in the way most boring to her and most irritating to Luca.

"We used to be friends."

"What kind of friends?"

"Not *that* kind. We were kids the last time I saw him."

"And he's been pining for you all this time? That's so romantic."

"It's not romantic, and he hasn't been pining. He tracked me down because it was beneficial for him to do so."

"Okay, beneficial how? He said you weren't poor. Oh my god, are you rich? Are you just, like, slumming it out here with the rest of us to stick it to your old man or something, and that's why you're so bad with people? Because you're used to being catered to?"

"What? No. Look, the place I grew up, it was basically run by six people. They said 'jump' and everyone jumped. Well, they decided they didn't like me anymore and wanted me gone. So my dad disowned me." It was the closest mortal equivalent to banishment I could come up with.

"Just like that? You guys didn't even have a falling out or anything?"

"No." My throat constricted, and I told myself it was from anger, not sadness. "We got along great before that."

"That's fucked up," Kurt offered.

"Thank you. It is. Though *some* people seem to think it's just fine." I glared at Luca. He glared back.

"I swear it's like he can hear you." Sonoma sighed. "He's too hot to be a bad guy."

Personally, I'd always found that a guy's chances of being a complete douche went up in tandem with his hotness.

"He's not a bad guy," I said finally. "Just a coward."

Luca's lips pressed into a thin line. He left soon after that. Once he was gone, it took a solid hour of me refusing to answer any more of Sonoma's questions before she finally stopped asking them. When my shift wound down and I walked out the back door, Luca was waiting for me.

"I'm not a coward." He shoved off the wall he'd been holding up and followed me across the employee parking lot.

"Whatever you need to tell yourself."

I often wondered what the coffee shop had been before its current incarnation, because the back was more like a courtyard than a parking lot, and one more at home in the forest than the desert. Non-native trees lined the perimeter. They had grown high, their branches spread wide to form a canopy over the small space. They cast the area in perpetual shadow, even in the cruelest heights of Phoenix summer.

Luca sped up and stepped in front of me, his eyes blazing. "I didn't just let you go, Ash."

"You weren't even there to say goodbye," I yelled, over a decade's worth of pent-up anger flooding out of me. "I'd have understood if you tried to come with me and they stopped you, but you didn't even show up. You *promised*. And you weren't there."

"Ash—"

"Do you have any idea what it was like for me? You can't live on your own here without an adult until you're eighteen. Somebody has to claim you. They make all of your decisions for you. I got shoved off on the people who wanted the money they got paid to take me because no one wanted me. I was just the crazy girl who was so traumatized by her daddy abandoning her that she made up a fictional world so she'd feel special.

"Without my Heartstone, I didn't have my abilities. I *wasn't* special. I started to think maybe I was crazy. Even when my powers started to trickle back in, part of me wondered if it was all in my head. Part of me *still* wonders that. Wonders if you aren't just a figment of my imagination I conjured up because my life sucks."

He listened to all of this with a look on his face I couldn't puzzle out. "I'm not in your head, Ash," he said softly.

Then he kissed me.

The touch of his lips was liquid fire, and the thrust of his tongue against mine spilled heat through me. He tasted like spice and midnight, a dark, heady mixture that made me press against him. His big hands slid around my waist, down my back and then lower, deliciously lower. I moaned into his mouth and deepened the kiss as his hands cupped my ass and squeezed.

If this was all in my head, I was doing a terrific job. I wanted to melt into him. I wanted to tear his clothes off and take him right there in the parking lot, as if fucking him would somehow make up for all of the shit I'd been through instead of just making everything worse.

I buried my fingers in his hair and climbed him, wrapped my legs around his waist. My weight didn't even shift him. He was strong and steady, his only reaction to pull me closer. Given where his hands were located, it ground my center against him.

I trailed my lips down his neck to lick the hollow at the juncture of his throat, and he growled in pleasure. I turned the lick to a nip, wanting to hear that deep male rumble again. But the next time Luca growled, it wasn't in pleasure, but in warning, his body tensing as he went alert.

I felt the cause of his shift in mood, the wrongness and corruption in the air. I flung myself off him, not wanting to be hindered by my limbs tangled up with his, when something dropped from the trees onto my neck.

I clawed at the thick, rubbery mass that wrapped around my throat, trying to gain enough purchase to pull it away. Its coils were easily two inches in diameter, the flesh soft and vaguely fuzzy, like the manta ray I'd once petted at the zoo.

Thuds sounded as more of the eel-like creatures fell from the trees. Solid black, the air around them hissed with curls of ebony smoke. They moved with eerie speed, snaking for me. The air crackled with the force of Luca's shift from human to wolf and he lunged, snapping the creatures up in his jaws. As his teeth cut clean through one, it turned entirely to smoke and vanished.

The creature around my throat tightened like a boa constrictor. Pressure built in my head and my vision went white. I got my fingers between the coils and my neck and pulled them away long enough to take a single, shuddering breath before it snapped tight around me again.

I fumbled for the dagger I always wore, the hip sheath hidden on the inside of my jeans, and pulled the blade free. Hacking the creature off me wasn't my first choice of action —I was just as likely to stab myself in the throat as I was to free myself—but since the alternative was dying, it was a choice I was willing to make.

I thrust the dagger straight through the middle of the coils. The creature shrieked, an ear-splitting noise, and sank a fanged mouth into my right shoulder. White-hot pain spilled through me.

Damn. I had really hoped it would poof into smoke like Luca's had done. Instead, it doubled down on constriction. Still, the attack had accomplished something. I knew where the beast's head was: locked onto my shoulder.

I reached up and clamped the creature's head with my right hand, drew my dagger up with the left and sliced its head off. Much like the proverbial chicken with its head cut off, the creature's body spasmed and flailed in its death throes. It had loosened up enough for me to breathe so I left it and whirled, searching for a new target.

There wasn't one. Luca had gone on a one-wolf killing spree and annihilated them, not a trace left save a lingering ribbon of black smoke. Which begged the question, why hadn't the one I'd killed disappeared like the others? Was it not dead enough?

Luca stalked toward me, shifted to human and pulled the creature off me with a growl that was still all wolf. He reached for the head and paused. It was still attached to my shoulder via what felt like two-inch-long fangs.

"Just do it," I said.

He put one hand on one side of the creature's mouth, one on the other, and pried its jaw open. I winced as the fangs slid out. Luca ripped the shoulder of my shirt off—yes, maybe the garment *had* already been ruined, but he could have asked first—and ran his fingers over the hot, swollen flesh.

"What the hell were those? And why didn't mine vanish like yours did?"

"Those were one of the Darkness' many forms. We call that particular form a Slither."

"Slither? Really?"

He let his shoulders rise and fall. "Sometimes when children name things, the name sticks."

"Okay. Slithers, then. Why is mine still here?"

Luca looked at the eel-like body on the asphalt. He still hadn't removed his hand from my shoulder. "It's still here," he said slowly, "because you killed it."

"You killed a ton of them. I don't see *their* bodies."

"I didn't kill them. I sent them back to where they came from. At least, that's our best guess on what happens to them." He looked at me with something akin to wonder on his face, like I was some great hope he hadn't actually believed in. "I *can't* kill them, Ash. No one in Elysium can. We fight them, and they become smoke and vanish, only to crawl back into our world the next day in another form.

"But *you* can. *Now* do you understand why you need to come home?"

Maybe I did, but I really didn't want to. I stared at the Slither on the ground. The voice of skepticism whispered that this could all be an elaborate trick. Illusion magic of some kind that had made Luca's monsters vanish when "killed" and made mine stick around.

The only problem was, I didn't know any magic that could make an illusion feel real enough to choke me, real enough to kill me.

"It's not my problem."

"It will *be* your problem if Elysium falls and the Darkness overruns the mortal world."

Part of me wondered if the mortal world might not deal with the Darkness just fine. They had tanks and guns and bombs, after all. Hell, I lived in Arizona. People here looked at you funny if you *didn't* own at least five firearms and more ammo than you could ever reasonably expect to shoot in one lifetime.

Of course, knowing what else I knew about the mortal world, if the Darkness unleashed itself here, every world superpower would likely choose another world superpower to blame for the problem, and the nuclear apocalypse would finally happen.

So yeah. Part of me wanted to just tell Luca to fuck off. Again. It wasn't as if I had some great affection for this place, some driving desire to save it from destruction. I didn't fit in here. I didn't belong.

I understood that some part of that failure was because I'd never really tried to fit in. I hadn't wanted to belong here, because Elysium owned my heart. It had broken it, too, and I'd never really healed. So maybe it was time to see if I *could* heal. Or if not, at least gain some kind of closure. Enough to let it go. Enough so that, if I left Elysium again, I could try to have an actual life here. Try to *be* someone here.

"I'm not promising you anything," I told Luca. "And I'm damn well not playing the part of Prophesied Savior of Elysium. But I'll come with you. I'll *see.*"

"That's all I'm asking."

"If I don't like what I see, I'm leaving again."

"Fair enough."

"Anything *else* I should know before you drop me in the fire?"

"Yes. I tried to get you to ask about it earlier. Your father's dying."

9

ASHLYNN

YOUR FATHER'S DYING.

I didn't know what to do with those words. My memories of my father were an incongruous disparity between the somewhat idyllic childhood I remembered and the cold viciousness with which he'd turned his back on me at the Oracle's proclamation.

Whatever my feelings were, I didn't have time to figure them out. I'd thought that going back to Elysium would involve physically traveling to a specific mortal locale that would let us cross over into that other realm. I'd also thought I'd get to go back to my apartment first, maybe pack some things. Instead, Luca simply spoke Elysium's name right there in the parking lot. I felt a flare of power from his glamoured Heartstone—I was still irritated that I couldn't see it, given how much he'd been naked around me—and the doorway appeared, an oval of Elysium shimmering into existence in the parking lot like a hologram image.

Luca retrieved the Slither's body, "As proof," he said, tossed it over his shoulder, and took my hand. Great. After twelve long years, I was going to walk into Elysium holding hands with a naked werewolf prince who had the dead body of a Dark eel-thing slung over his shoulders like a hunting trophy.

At least I wasn't barefoot and pregnant.

We stepped through and the magic of Elysium's border slipped over me. I felt its confusion, as if it recognized me or my power, and yet it simultaneously wanted to deny me passage because I didn't possess my Heartstone. But Luca possessed his, and I was touching him, so it allowed me to cross over.

The change hit me with vicious abruptness the moment I breathed in Elysian air. Power tore through my body, drove me to my knees as the truth of my heritage sank into me.

I was from the Hunter territory, and it was rumored my father's line went back to Artemis herself. As the strength in my muscles doubled, the weaknesses the mortal world had wrought upon my body fleeing in the wake of my birthright, I could almost believe that rumor.

The blood in my veins practically hummed. Even breathing felt easier, more right somehow, and in that moment I wasn't thinking about banishment or betrayal or the Darkness. All that I was, all that existed, was the joy in my veins, the sense of utter rightness coursing through me.

How? How had I managed so long in the mortal world? How had I even considered not coming back to this?

My exuberance must have shown on my face because Luca grinned at me, a large, wolfish baring of teeth, and I saw my old friend in it.

"Race you to Summit Rock," he challenged. The wolf tore out of him in a fraction of a second, far less time than it had taken him in the mortal world, and I yelled curses at him as his paws dug into the earth and I tore off after him.

He'd brought us back to Elysium in the same meadow where we'd spent so many of our childhood summers, when we were young enough that something like winning a race to the rock at the top of Wolf Mountain was still a bragging right worth having.

Now, like then, I ran for the pure glory of it. A mountain was nothing to me here, nothing to the muscles that bunched and released, propelling me up the narrow dirt path, letting me dodge the clods of dirt Luca's massive paws flung down behind him.

I wouldn't win, not following in his wake. The path twisted and turned too frequently, was too narrow to let me overtake him. So I didn't try. I followed him up and fifty feet from the top I leapt off the path, grabbing hold of the sheer, vertical rock face that led to the top and Summit Rock. If I lost my grip, it was a fall of a few hundred feet to the bottom.

I might not survive that, even being what I was in Elysium. I didn't care, was too exhilarated to care.

My fingers caught rock and dug in, sharp edges tearing into the soft flesh of my palms. I ignored the pain and scrambled up, fingers and toes finding purchase, and dragged my way to the top as fast as I dared. My hands finally grabbed the lip of the summit, and I hauled myself up onto the flat rock at the mountain's peak...at the same damn exact moment Luca jumped onto it from the path, his paws landing with a soft thud.

"I won," I said, panting from the exertion.

He shifted from wolf to human in a blink. "We tied."

"No, you sprung the race on me *and* jumped the gun, therefore I was at an unfair disadvantage, therefore I won."

"Do those excuses fly in the mortal world?" he taunted.

"I don't know, what's your excuse for having a head start, four paws, and still only managing to tie me?"

"Being a gentleman?" he offered.

I snorted. "If you're a gentleman, I'm a fragile fucking flower."

He laughed. It was a deeper version of the laugh I remembered, but it fit right into me like it always had, his laughter and his place by my side something I'd taken for granted until it wasn't there anymore.

I blinked and turned away from him, swinging my legs over the side of Summit Rock to look down on Elysium. We were on the northern-most edge of the island, and I could hear the crash of waves behind us. Before me, the meadow spread out. On the western edge it gave way to the White Woods, where Luca's pack held territory, and on the eastern edge to the darkness of the Dragons' Black Caverns. Before I'd lived in the mortal world, I'd had no idea how much those territory names sounded like stock fairy tale places, and it amused me now.

The amusement faded as I looked south, to the center of the island, where the hexagram of Elysium lay at the bottom of a deep valley. It was stamped into the earth like a brand, large and imposing, two hundred feet from the tip of one star point to the opposite tip of another.

In my youth, it had been the purest iridescent silver stone. Now, from this vantage point, I could see it was shot through with veins of black that mottled the perfection.

"The Darkness," Luca said, dropping down—naked again—beside me.

I almost rolled my eyes. As if I'd *needed* him to point out that the corruption in Elysium's hexagram was Darkness-related.

"How far has it spread?" I asked, all the while telling myself that I didn't care. I didn't care how much it had infected, didn't care how many people it had hurt, didn't care what was being done to stop it.

I'd always been a bad liar, even to myself. Because now that I was *here* again, my heart and body—traitors, both of them—wouldn't stop shouting their joy at being *home*. A handful of minutes here and already I knew I would never willingly return to the mortal realm, that I couldn't endure the rest of my life there, trying to eek out an existence as a shadow of my true self.

And I told myself that that was okay. It wasn't as if the land itself had betrayed me. It wasn't *Elysium* that had forsaken me. Only her people, and I didn't have to forgive those people to live here. Better to be alone here than alone *there*.

Except Luca's presence beside me reminded me that I wasn't alone. I wanted to pretend I'd never been banished, that he hadn't betrayed me, so I wouldn't feel bad about how easy it was to be around him again.

"It's been sighted in every territory on the island, now." Luca said, reminding me that I'd asked him a question. "The closer you get to the hexagram, the more dangerous it is. That break in the center" —he pointed at the thick black vein running through the hexagram's heart— "appeared the day they sent you away."

I noticed how he said *they* instead of *we*. Remembered how he'd said he hadn't wanted to let me go. His hand was less than a centimeter from mine and I lifted my fingers to brush the thick scar circling his wrist.

His breathing quickened, just the slightest hitch.

"Luca?" I whispered.

"Hmm?"

"The day it happened. Did something—was there—"

The sound of a blade whistling through the air cut off a sentence I didn't want to finish anyway. I dropped flat and the blade bit through the air where my head had been a split second before. My Elysium-born Hunter reflexes kicked in and I grabbed the hilt of the blade, snatching it out of the air.

I flipped around and rolled to my knees in one fluid movement and sent the dagger flying back at the person who'd thrown it. For all the werewolf—and she *had* to be a werewolf, because nothing else moved quietly enough to sneak up on both Luca and me—had maintained stealth in her assent to Summit Rock, she hadn't bothered to try and hide, and the dagger buried itself in her abdomen with a deep thunk.

Surprise spread across her face—what the fuck had she expected, anyway?—and I leapt to my feet and tackled her. A knife wound to the gut might hurt like a bitch but it wouldn't keep a werewolf down for long. Though it seemed to be keeping this one down longer than it should.

Strangely, she didn't fight me as I ripped it from her stomach and held it to her throat. She didn't even look at me, just turned her gaze left, to Luca.

"Don't kill her, Ash," he said. It wasn't a command, it was a request.

"What the *fuck?*" I asked the oddly pliant werewolf beneath me. But for all she'd just tried to kill me, she still didn't bother to acknowledge my existence.

"I had to know if she was worth it," she said to Luca, and there was a world of bitterness in her voice.

"Hey," I slid the dagger up, pressed the tip just below her eye socket. *That* finally got her attention. Her gut wound might be healing—still slower than it should be, I noted—but if I popped her eyeball out, she wasn't growing that back. Ever. "Person you just tried to kill here. I repeat my *what the fuck?*"

"You should have stayed gone," she snarled. "You get everything, you *always* got everything."

If I said *what the fuck* again I'd be a broken record.

"Yeah, banishment was a real fucking delight, do I know you?"

For a woman with a knife to her eyeball she somehow managed a condescending sneer. "Of course you wouldn't remember. But then, Barren Hunter's perfect daughter never had to notice anyone else. Not when she had the entire Hunter territory's adoration and the pack prince's attention."

There *was* something vaguely familiar about her petulant nature. I looked her over. Brown hair a shade or two lighter than mine, pale green eyes. There was no doubt she was prettier than me in the classic sense, more feminine, more shapely. She easily had two cup sizes on me, I mean, for love of the mortals' Jesus, did werewolves have to get all the looks?

I leaned in to sniff her—I might not have a werewolf's sense of smell, but I was a Hunter, and our noses were better than any race's save the wolves. I breathed deep, smelled honeysuckle and...Luca.

My brain came to a screeching halt as irrational jealousy overtook it. If I could have growled like a wolf, I would have then. Fortunately, I couldn't, because reason nudged its way into my brain.

So what if he'd been fucking Kiera—*that* was her name, she'd always smelled cloyingly sweet—and recently, too, given how all over her his scent was? Screwing was practically the national pastime of unmated werewolves, and it was certainly none of my business.

I didn't need this. I hadn't come back here to end up in the middle of a domestic dispute between wolves, and I was absolutely certain the pinch in my chest had something to do with my recently-returned powers and nothing to do with that incessant voice in the back of my head whispering that I should rip Kiera's throat out because Luca was *mine*.

He wasn't mine. *I* wasn't a mated werewolf for Darkness sake.

I shoved off Kiera in disgust. "Whatever lover's spat you two are having, work it out without me. And Kiera? You ever attack me again and I'll put a silver arrow through your eye from the other side of the fucking island."

I turned and walked to the edge of the cliff that faced the sea. Screw Luca. Screw werewolves in general. I'd come here to feel alive again, and I knew just how to do it. I backed up ten paces, took a running start, and threw myself off the cliff-side, ignoring Luca's startled shout.

Cold wind whipped through my hair, my heart a fast pulse behind my chest as I plummeted, the ocean surface rapidly approaching. I put my hands together in a classic dive pose and plunged into the waters.

Icy perfection hit my body, a welcome relief after the desert heat of Phoenix. I opened my eyes to the neon colors of the ocean flora and fauna, let the dive carry me as deep as it would before my lungs started to protest. Then I turned and kicked my way to the surface, inhaling great lungfuls of air, a stupid smile on my face. The smile stayed there, right up until the moment Luca splashed into the water ten feet from me.

10

LUCA

I saw what Ash was going to do the second she started walking backwards.

"Ash, don't!" She didn't listen. The Darkness-cursed daredevil sprinted and flung herself off Summit Rock, and if she didn't jump far enough she would hit the bloody rocks instead of the ocean.

I stalked after her but Kiera grabbed my arm.

"Let go," I ordered. I would have simply shoved her off, but I was trying hard to have sympathy for her. I'd broken things off with her months ago, when I'd still thought of our encounters as harmless fun but realized she was angling for a mating bond.

I didn't harbor any illusions that she was in love with me—Kiera had always been interested in one thing from me aside from sex, and that was my position in the pack—but I *had* been more or less monogamous while we'd been together. It had been laziness on my end, but she'd thought it meant something, so I'd ended things.

She hadn't taken it well, and she'd made it apparent, at every opportunity she got, that she thought I would change my mind. After the Oracle had named me as the one to bring Ashlynn back, I'd come home to find Kiera in my bed. I'd promptly thrown her out, but if the smell of her was any indication, she'd been in it again last night, and I didn't doubt she'd orchestrated the whole thing just so Ashlynn would smell me on her.

I was going to have to put locks on the damn house, which would make me the first werewolf in the history of werewolves to have door locks.

"Why? So you can go after your one true love?" Kiera said, her voice layered in false honey. "If the looks of things are any indication, she doesn't want you. I do."

"You don't want me, you want to be pack princess. I've already explained that's never going to happen."

"Have you even told her?" Kiera snapped.

"Let. Go."

"You haven't, have you?" She laughed. "You've got scars for her and she doesn't even know. Do you think she'll give you a pity fuck if you tell her?"

I ripped my arm out of her grasp, done being sympathetic. "Ashlynn is none of your business. And if you ever attempt to harm her again, I'll rip your throat out myself."

I turned and launched myself after Ashlynn.

The water was absolutely frigid, but that didn't stop Ash from having a grin on her face. One that died the second she caught sight of me. As if I'd sucked all the fun out of her near-death dive by coming after her, she turned and kicked for the shore without a single word to me.

I followed her out of the ocean, and the only reason my teeth didn't chatter as the wind whipped around us was because it was decidedly unmanly for a werewolf prince's teeth to do so. I was cold and pissed off.

"Are you trying to get yourself killed?" I demanded.

She rolled her eyes. "Please, I could have cleared that

jump in my sleep." Ash seemed to hold herself to the were-wolf prince code about showing weakness, because even though her lips were blue and the careful formation of her words indicated they were numb as well, she clenched her fists to keep from visibly shivering.

I wanted to take her in my arms and rub some warmth into her, but I didn't think she'd appreciate it. "Let's go, before you catch your damn death."

"Don't you have a werewolf bitch to fuck into a better mood?"

Well, now, that response was unexpected. "Why, Ash? Jealous?"

"As if."

She was, I realized. She *was* jealous. Maybe Kiera's little stunt had an upside after all. "I haven't been with Kiera in months."

She shrugged, the movement stiff with cold. "Not my business. You can fuck whoever you want."

"I can, but I haven't." I suddenly wanted to be very, very clear about that fact.

"She smells like she rolled in you."

"She has a problem with breaking and entering. Can we go now? I'm fucking freezing."

I didn't wait for a reply. I shrugged off my human skin for the more insulating wolf and its attendant fur. The shift rid me of some of the cold, returning feeling to previously numb extremities. Ash didn't have that luxury, and the third time she fell on the climb up from the ocean I pinned her, growled at her, and nodded at my back.

"N-not, h-happening," she said, unable to keep her teeth from chattering at this point.

I growled at her again. If she didn't get on, this walk was going to take all day.

"S-still, n-not, happening."

I licked her face. It scrunched up adorably in response.

"What the f-fuck, Luca?"

I licked her again, nodded at my back again.

"S-seriously? Your brilliant plan is to lick me until I get on?"

If I had a brilliant plan, it would be to get us warm, shift back to human, and lick her somewhere else until she got on me somewhere else.

But that was neither here nor there.

ASHLYNN

AFTER THE FOURTH PASS OF SLOBBERY WEREWOLF TONGUE I gave in and got on Luca's back. Yes, werewolves were as large as ponies, but they really weren't as well-designed for riding. And frankly, before this moment, if you'd put *riding* and *Luca* together in the same sentence, it would have conjured up a very different image for me.

Thankfully, I was so cold, and still weirdly pissed about Kiera, that it didn't take much effort to get my mind out of the damn gutter. I buried my fingers in Luca's thick fur and let his body heat take the numb away. I hadn't thought to ask *where* we were going, but as he reached the top of the cliffs and started down the other side, it was clear we were heading for pack territory.

I was in no mood to be reintroduced to the White Woods pack. They'd been like a second family to me once, and whatever their response to my return was going to be, I wasn't interested in warm welcomes or frigid stares, or anything at all from them, really.

It was a relief when Luca simply skirted the edge of the woods and walked up to a lone cabin. I clambered off him and he shifted to human and opened the front door. I'd forgotten werewolves didn't bother with locks.

I darted past him, too cold at this point to care about anything other than getting out of the wind.

My teeth chattered and it felt like every muscle in my body had seized up. I couldn't make myself regret jumping into the ocean, though. That one reckless act had made me feel more like myself than I had in years, and it wasn't like I would die of hypothermia. Not in Elysium.

But I could be really, really miserable from it, and possibly sick for a few days.

Luca slammed the door shut behind us, took one look at me, and muttered a string of curses. He herded me out of the living room and through a door into the bathroom.

"Take your clothes off," he snapped, turning the shower on full-blast.

"Y-you w-wish," I stuttered through chattering teeth. It was pure spite though—my clothes were soaked through and freezing—and I kicked my shoes off, unzipped my jeans and then fumbled at the button, trying to get my unfeeling fingers to open the damn thing.

Luca solved the problem by ripping them off. Damn, but that could have been *so* sexy if I wasn't so very, very cold. He reached for my shirt. Panic flared in my chest and I batted his hand away.

"You're freezing," he ground out, "and you didn't seem to have any issues being naked in front of me this morning."

I shrugged. This morning I'd had makeup covering the tattoo of his name. If my dip in the ocean hadn't removed it, the shower certainly would.

He reached for the hem of my shirt again and I shoved him back.

Oddly, the expression on his face softened.

"I know you cover your scar, Ash. You should know it doesn't matter to me."

My Heartstone scar. He thought I was covering my Heartstone scar. I preferred him to hold on to that theory rather than guess the truth.

"I'm n-not taking the sh-shirt off."

"Fine." He grabbed me around the waist and pulled me into the shower with him. I yelped as the hot water hit like knives against my too-cold skin. Luca wrapped himself around me, shielding me from the disparity between my internal temperature and the water, his body heat warming me as the shower filled with the delicious warmth of steam.

My toes and fingers burned as sensation returned to them, and all through it Luca held me to him. He held me until I quit shivering, continued to hold me until I was warm enough to relax against him, to appreciate the hands he rubbed over me as something other than a means of providing friction for the purpose of warming me up.

He noticed the change in me and his hands switched to a slow, lazy roving.

"Before Kiera showed up, you were going to ask me something," he said softly. "What was it?"

"I don't remember," I lied. My bravery in wanting to know the truth had disappeared somewhere between then and now.

"Liar," he whispered, and nipped gently at my earlobe.

It sent a zing through the entirety of my half-naked body, and I was suddenly very aware of all the places my skin touched his.

"Luca," I whispered, and I wasn't sure if it was a question, a plea, or a refusal.

"Ashlynn," he replied, his voice a silky rumble in my ear. God, I loved the way he said my name. His hands slipped under my shirt, skimmed up my stomach and stopped just beneath my breasts.

"Yes?" he asked.

I reminded myself that I had never been one of those people who equated sex with love. I wanted Luca. It didn't have to mean anything if I had him. "Hell yes."

He chuckled and his hands closed around my breasts, thumbs flicking across nipples already gone stiff. I moaned and ground back on him, felt him harden against my backside in response. I had the feeling this was a very bad idea, but when he sucked my earlobe into his mouth and flicked my nipples again, I didn't care.

I turned in the circle of his arms and took his lower lip into my mouth, rolling it between my teeth. He made a low, rough growl and backed me against the shower wall. When I released his lip he claimed my mouth, thrusting his tongue through lips I was only too willing to part for him.

He returned one hand to teasing my breast, the other tracing a line down my stomach. His fingers slipped inside my panties. When they touched my hot, aching center he groaned and bit my neck.

"You're so fucking wet," he said, and plunged his fingers into me. I couldn't stop my hips from jerking forward, from grinding my clit against his palm. He worked me with his hand and I obligingly moved against him, couldn't have stopped myself from moving, the rhythm he set one I was incapable of not matching.

He dipped his head, took my nipple in his mouth in a deep pull, the sensation of it through the thin layers of my shirt and bra excruciatingly delicious. I ground against him, frantic for release, as he nipped his way up my collarbone, back up my neck.

"Say my name, Ash," he whispered. His thumb found my clit and I didn't say his name—I screamed it as I came apart in his arms, my pussy spasming around his fingers still buried inside me.

I was drunk on him, could barely see straight as I came down from the high. He slipped his fingers from me and kissed me again. His tongue coaxed my mouth open, and I reached down between us to take his length in my hand. He was thick and hard, and I savored the feel of him when he groaned and pushed himself against my palm.

A knock sounded loudly on the door of the cabin.

"Fuck," Luca said.

I was of half a mind to keep playing with Luca until he forgot the person at the door, and they went away.

"Luca!" The name was half bark, half growl, and all command. I knew that voice, and it dumped cold water on my lust.

Some people got turned on by the thrill of discovery, but I was not one of them. Especially when the person currently yelling like he owned the damn forest—which he technically did—was Luca's father. Since it didn't sound like he'd softened any in his old age, I knew if Luca didn't get the door in the next minute, Aiden Ferrar would simply barrel through it.

"We're not finished here," Luca told me. He punctuated the declaration with a quick, rough kiss and stepped out of the shower, ripping a towel off the rack and throwing it around his waist as he stalked for the door.

I stayed in the shower because the hot water had not yet run out, and because it was as good of an excuse as any not to interact with the leader of the White Woods pack. He'd never had a real problem with me, per se, but he'd never appreciated my smart mouth, either.

I canted my head, listening. Werewolf residences tended to be built rather soundproof, for obvious reasons, but if Luca left the door open—the door slammed shut.

Damn it.

❧ 12 ❧

LUCA

As usual, my father had impeccable timing. Impeccably *bad* timing.

"You're supposed to be bringing Ashlynn to the Elders, not fucking her," he snarled. Snarling was what he did best. He was a walking, talking, alpha-type werewolf cliché.

I leaned back against the door and crossed my arms, as if I couldn't care less what he thought. Mostly, because I couldn't.

"On the contrary, I thought the Elders *wanted* me to fuck her. However will their Oracle's prophecy play out if she doesn't want a mating bond with me?"

"You know damn well they wanted her brought to them as soon as you found her. And as for the *other*, the choice isn't up to her."

The change rippled beneath my skin, seeking release I denied it, and I shoved off the wall before I could think better of it. I wasn't thinking at all.

There were a number of ways for Elysians to declare a partnership. Some were as basic as the mortals' marriages. The truest form was a melding of Heartstones—an Elysian could remove their own Heartstone without the damage and scarring caused to Ashlynn by its forceful removal, and split that Heartstone in two.

A freely given half of a Heartstone would meld to the one it was given to, and when two lovers exchanged halves, they each gained a new whole, a blended whole. *That* could never be forced—a Heartstone could only be safely broken by the person to whom it belonged. But a werewolf's mating bond was a different story.

At our base nature, domination was a part of every werewolf, male or female. The stronger we were, the more compelled we felt to push that drive. It was why so many assholes ended up in power. Prime example: my father.

The mating bond was another extension of that need to dominate. When a bond occurred between two equals, it wasn't a problem. There was a give and take, a mutual respect. When it didn't? It was terrible. A strong enough werewolf could force that bond on someone else. That, in itself, was illegal under pack law, and the penalty was death.

The real problem came in the gray areas of the law. Which was that the magic of the mating bond could, in the onset of new love or the drive of lust, misconstrue desire as consent. Pack law *considered* it consent and the bond legitimate. Which was why most werewolves guarded their emotions fiercely, and mating bonds were rare. Those who chose a mating bond usually only did so after years of trust.

Because the only way to break a mating bond was if one of the partners died.

"I'll never force a bond on her."

"Then you're a fool. And someone else will."

I almost went for his throat right then. If another pack member succeeded in forcing a bond on Ash, they could *make* her break her Heartstone.

"The Oracle named *me*."

"Because you told him to." My surprise must have shown on my face, because my father laughed. "No one else knows, if that's what you're worried about. But I'm not an idiot. I knew when the Oracle said he'd bring them back you wouldn't leave your precious Ashlynn in anyone else's care."

His hands shifted to claws, made me aware my own claws were out.

"You want to redeem yourself, son? Get her to bond with you. I don't care how you do it. I won't have the pack lose the Elders' favor because of your precious morals. And if you don't? Maybe your little subterfuge with the Oracle comes to light. Maybe it turns out he meant to name someone else for her. Maybe that person was me.

"You think you're the only person who can turn a woman's head with lust until she doesn't know *yes* from *no*? Maybe *I'll* fuck her senseless until she—"

Fury hazed my vision with red. Any sense I had that would have told me my father was only taunting me went right out of my head. I didn't care what his reasons were. No one, not even the pack alpha, was going to talk about Ash that way.

The wolf tore out of me and I lunged for Aiden's throat.

ASHLYNN

Not even the soundproofing on the house could block the roar and growl of fighting werewolves. My heart thudded in my chest and I sprinted for the door.

Werewolves fought all the time. It was natural for them, a release of pent-up energy and adrenaline. But they didn't fight the pack alpha. Outside of very carefully moderated sparring bouts the entire pack kept an eye on, a fight against the alpha was considered a challenge to pack leadership. And those challenges always ended in someone's death.

I flung the door open and ran outside, my dagger in hand, unwilling to name the fear that caught in my throat at the sight of Luca's white-silver wolf battling his father's dark brown. Blood spattered Luca's white fur, and I didn't need either of them to tell me this wasn't a friendly match.

Luca's attention shifted briefly to me, and it was enough of a distraction that Aiden's jaws locked on Luca's throat.

No. *No.* I didn't know what had possessed Luca to get into a fight with his father, but I wasn't going to sit here and watch Luca die. He was the only person on this damn island I could stand to be around, and I told myself that *that* was the only reason I did the dumbest thing I've ever done in my life.

I sprinted down the porch steps, Hunter strength and speed in my veins, and tackled the alpha of the White Woods pack.

I hit him with enough force to knock him off Luca and to the ground, but I had enough good sense not to try and pin him. I might be Hunter strong, but humans didn't fare well against werewolf claws. I tumbled away from him and rolled to my feet.

Aiden gained four paws and unleashed a growl of sufficiently scary alpha proportions right in my face. Luca's muscles bunched and he launched himself into the air, landing between me and Aiden.

Stupid idiot wolf. Elysians lived and breathed the goddamn Oracle's prophecies. None of them were going to kill *me*. I shoved myself back in front of him.

"What the hell are you two *doing*?"

Aiden growled again and shifted back to his human form, a sneer on his lips as his gaze swiped over me. In all fairness, I must look ridiculous. I'd laid my wet clothes on top of the wood-burning stove in the living room to dry, so I'd shrugged into one of Luca's shirts I'd scrounged from a drawer. He was massively larger than I was, so there'd been no hope of his sweatpants fitting me, and while the shirt covered the important bits, it didn't do much else for me.

Luca lunged forward and I shoved back against his chest with all my Hunter-born strength.

"It's a good thing one of you two has a fucking brain," Aiden snarled. "Make it happen, Luca. Or I *will* take the choice away from you. And take her to the Elders in the next half hour or I'll have the entire damn pack escort you there."

The low growl that had been a constant rumble in Luca's

throat during the entire conversation didn't cease until Aiden disappeared from both sight and scent.

I turned and shoved Luca right in his furry chest. "Are you trying to get yourself killed?"

Luca was strong, but Aiden was too, and from what I remembered of Luca's father, the White Woods alpha was vicious.

Luca snapped back to human. Gashes rent his throat and abdomen, the wounds closing over with the preternatural speed werewolves healed with.

"He deserved it," was Luca's brilliant defense.

"He *deserved it*?" I repeated. "You just challenged your fucking alpha. If he wanted to, this wouldn't end until one of you was dead."

As much as I would like to think Aiden wouldn't force his son into a death match, I had no idea if it was true. "Scary" and "bastard" were the two words I remembered being used most often to describe the White Woods alpha, usually together.

Luca shrugged.

"What was that about?" I demanded.

Another shrug. He was loquacious, my wolf.

No. Not *my* wolf. Not *my* fucking anything.

"You used to toe the line pretty hard where he was concerned." It had always irritated me, how deferential Luca was to his father, tip-toeing around him all the time. I was the one always pissing the old man off.

"That was before you left." He walked past me, up the front porch steps, as if nothing unusual had occurred. I followed.

"What did he mean by *make it happen*? What choice?"

"Nothing. He didn't mean anything." Luca kept walking, to all appearances unconcerned, but tension lined his shoulders, and he wouldn't meet my gaze. If I had come back in the middle of a pack power struggle, I wanted to know.

"He meant *something*," I insisted, following him into the bedroom where he dragged on pants and a shirt. "Did something happen between you and the pack? Why are you living way out here on the outskirts of White Woods territory?"

He ignored me.

"*Look* at me." I grabbed his arm. Luca whirled on me and we were across the room in a blink, my back against the wall, Luca's hands pinning mine above my head.

There was something in his eyes, something hot and needy and almost panicked. He closed them and rubbed his cheek against mine, buried his face in the crook of my neck and breathed me in. He was acting like a—well, like a mated wolf whose partner had just been attacked and he now had a desperate need to know I was okay.

Which was all kinds of ridiculous. One, because we definitely weren't mated—one orgasm did not a lifelong commitment make—and two, I hadn't been attacked so...what the hell was going on?

I tried to make sense out of it. Luca had claimed me a long time ago as his friend. Yes, I held a grudge against him, but that didn't mean he held the same against me, so it was very possible he still thought of me as family. Good werewolves were protective of family.

Clearly, Luca was supposed to have taken me directly to the Elders on arriving with me, and he hadn't. It had obviously pissed Aiden off. Maybe he'd said something about me that Luca had construed as a threat.

A threat to his *friend*, not to his *mate*.

This was fine. All I needed to do was calm him down.

"Everything's fine," I murmured, in my best soothe-the-werewolf voice. "Whatever Aiden said—it doesn't matter."

His father's name elicited another growl, but he dropped

my hands in favor of closing his around my waist and pulling me to him. I tried to convince myself it was a nice, chaste hug, but well, it wasn't.

"Don't trust the pack, Ash."

"What?" Those were the last words I'd ever have expected to come out of his mouth. "Why?"

He shook his head. "The Darkness—it has everyone on edge. Everyone's lost someone and everyone's looking for an answer. Right now they're looking to you. But you of all people know how easily they can turn on you if they don't like what they find."

"You're not making any sense." I rubbed at the tense muscles in his back to take the sting out of my words. Damn it, now I was the one acting like a mated fucking wolf. But I couldn't for the life of me make myself stop touching him. He felt good. Solid. Real. And I'd been alone for a very long time. It was okay to want to lean on him for the moment. Natural, even. It didn't mean anything.

"I know, just—be careful around the other wolves, okay?"

"Okay." It wasn't like I'd had any intention of going to the pack's weekend bonfire anyway.

"And maybe don't believe everything you hear about me." He let go of me abruptly. "I'll go see if your clothes are dry."

He walked out, leaving me to wonder just what I could expect to hear about him.

Where had the scars on his wrists come from? Why was the pack prince living on the outskirts of his own territory and getting into pissing matches with his father? What was it about me coming home that Luca didn't want to tell me?

🦋   14   🦋

ASHLYNN

My clothes were only partially dry, the button on my jeans was gone, and the fabric was stiff with sea salt, but anything was better than going to meet the Elders wearing Luca's clothes. I wanted to delay meeting the Elders entirely, but Luca was still weirdly on-edge.

Besides, while we might be leaving in time to avoid Aiden's promise of a full pack escort, we did open the door to find one solitary pack member on Luca's porch. If the wealth of red hair didn't give away his identity, the ever-present smirk on his face would have done it.

"Gareth?"

Luca's best friend and the resident pack trickster grinned. "Hey, little Ash. I had to come see if it was really you."

"Who else would it be? And I'm not little anymore." Before I could remember that I was mad at him and everyone else on this damn island I jumped off the porch and flung myself into his arms. He caught me and twirled me in a circle before setting me down.

"Easy, killer. I know I'm sinfully attractive, but never let it be said I encroach on another man's territory."

"You're not *that* attractive," I said. Though in all fairness, he really was. "And whose territory precisely do you think you're encroaching on?"

He looked confused. "Luca's, obviously. I always knew you two would get together."

"We're not together," I said shortly. Maybe I couldn't keep my hands off the man but that was neither here nor there. I was allowed to have a wildly physical attraction to him without it being anything more.

I'd expected the statement to be all that was needed to get Gareth to drop the subject—he was hardly the pack matchmaker—but instead confusion spread across his face and he looked at Luca.

"But you were supp—"

"You heard her," Luca said, cutting him off. "We're not together."

Gareth weirdly looked like he wanted to argue.

"Is there a reason you're so interested in my love life?" I asked.

He looked from me to Luca, then back. "No?"

"Convincing."

"It's just, the Darkness—"

"*Gareth*," Luca growled, the two syllables all the warning it took to snap Gareth's mouth shut.

Even with Luca cutting him off, Gareth's mention of the Darkness made it dawn on me why Luca might have been the one sent to come find me. Yeah, we had history, and that would make me more likely to trust him, but the pack might have sent him for a more calculated reason.

Luca was the heir to the White Woods pack. If my status hadn't shifted in my absence, I was still the heir to the Hunter territory. Our respective territories neighbored each other, and pack and Hunter had always had an uneasy relationship. With the Darkness presenting a common danger, maybe Aiden had decided an official alliance with the Hunters would be to the pack's benefit.

And what better way to secure an alliance than the time-honored tradition of marrying your kids off to each other? No wonder Luca had practically thrown himself at me the moment we reconnected. Suddenly Aiden's cryptic order to "make it happen" made sense.

No wonder Kiera had been pissed about me coming home. If she'd been in Luca's bed regularly she'd probably thought the position of pack princess was hers for the taking. Maybe Luca had wanted it to be. Obviously, the fact that he hadn't mentioned any of this to me, and the fact his father wasn't happy with him, meant he didn't want this. Didn't want *me*.

Well, fucking fine. I didn't want him either. I just wished I hadn't teased him and let him get me off in the shower. Clearly, he'd only been fucking me because he was ordered to.

Had he been thinking about Kiera when he touched me? Kiera, with her perfect curves and her breasts that were twice the size of mine? Yeah, she was a bitch, but I'd discovered years ago that a lot of men didn't really care about that. Who would have thought Luca would be one of them?

"We should go." I set off ahead of Luca and Gareth. I was suddenly *dying* to meet the Elders. Anything to get my mind off the fact that, not only had Luca *not* come for me when I was banished, he hadn't even come for me now for any other reason than familial pack duty. And he'd clearly hit his limit on that if he wanted away from me so badly he'd gotten into a physical fight with Aiden.

I couldn't believe I'd almost asked him about the scars. Asked him if he *had* tried to come for me that day and someone had stopped him. Would he have lied to me? Made up some story, any story, that would make me forgive him? Would I have tumbled right into his bed? Let him fuck me and say all the right things until being mated to him seemed like a perfectly reasonable thing to do?

"Ash!" Gareth and Luca called after me in unison. It sounded like they were still on Luca's porch—I didn't bother turning around to see.

"What?" I yelled back. "I'm off to learn about my glorious destiny. Isn't that what everyone wants from me?"

LUCA

GARETH MIGHT BE MY BEST FRIEND, BUT AT THE MOMENT he was on the list of people I could cheerfully murder. He'd spooked the hell out of Ashlynn, if the rigorous pace she set in the general direction of the Elders' castle was any indication.

If I'd thought she'd been warming to me, if I'd thought maybe she *could* want me after all, I'd been wrong. Gareth's mere mention of us as a couple had made her shut down. Maybe she'd been up for a quick fuck earlier, but now that mention of an actual relationship had been made, all lust had left her. I doubted she'd let me touch her like that again.

And damn it, I was hard just *thinking* about touching her like that again. Given where we were going, I needed to get my mind off her. Or at least off having my fingers inside her.

Think about something else. Think about my father. Nothing killed lust like thinking about your asshole dad. I wondered how long I had before he tried to force the issue of the mating bond. If I didn't fulfill the requirements of the Oracle's prophecy soon, I had no doubt that Aiden would go to the Oracle and try to convince him to renounce me as Ashlynn's mate.

I just didn't think he'd succeed. Because when I'd ordered the Oracle to name me as Ashlynn's mate, he'd laughed at me. Laughed, and shown me the written prophecy, where my name was already inked next to hers. I refused to dwell too much on that fact. But whether my father tried to usurp the Oracle's will or didn't, if he or any other member of the pack were to succeed in forging a mating bond with Ash, it might make the Elders reconsider everything.

And while my father had to know his chances of seducing Ashlynn were low and he'd likely only said it to set me off, the pack didn't exactly have a dearth of young, attractive men without scruples. Which was why I had to make sure Ashlynn stayed far, far away from the pack.

Gareth was about the only wolf in the whole territory I trusted.

"She seems pissed," Gareth said, his voice softer than a whisper. Werewolves learned to speak at a volume that was practically sub-audible. It was the only way to have a private conversation from other werewolves or Hunters without having to put fifty feet between you and them.

I responded at the same volume. "That's because she *is* pissed, genius."

"You didn't tell her? About the prophecy?"

"I told her. I left out the part where I'm supposedly her destined mate. It seemed like a lot to shove on a person."

"I wouldn't think she'd have minded all *that* much. I wasn't kidding earlier. I did always think you two would end up together. Everyone did. Hell, since you're only three years older than her there was a betting pool on whether you'd wait to lose your virginity until she was old enough to do the honors."

I shot him a glare.

"What? You know the pack. We'll bet on anything. You can't seriously expect me to believe the sparks haven't flown at least a little?"

"Believe it. She hates my fucking guts."

"What for?"

"I made her a promise and I broke it."

"She can't be holding that against you. Your dad put you in silver chains for trying to stop her banishment."

I didn't say anything.

"Shit. She doesn't know about that either, does she?"

"No," I said shortly, "and you're not going to tell her."

"Why the fuck not? She deserves to know you didn't abandon her."

Because I have no interest in coercing her. "Don't tell her. That's an order."

I rarely pulled pack rank. I never pulled it with Gareth.

"Just so you know, Your Royal Highness, you're a flaming idiot."

"Noted."

❧ 16 ❧

ASHLYNN

I'D INTENDED TO HEAD STRAIGHT TO THE ELDERS' CASTLE, but Luca insisted on a short detour to retrieve the dead Slither body from the bottom of Summit Rock. He'd dropped it earlier in his haste to race me to the top, and insisted retrieving it was worth delaying for now. By the way Gareth *oohed* and *ahed* over it before Luca shoved it in a bag, apparently it was.

I didn't care. I was still pissed and embarrassed and all I wanted was to find out what the Elders wanted from me so I could tell them no. Then I'd demand my Heartstone back and be on my merry way to...somewhere. I hadn't thought that far ahead yet. Was there another hermit's cabin like Luca's on the outskirts of some territory sitting abandoned, waiting for me to claim? I could spend the rest of my days sitting in a rocking chair with a sword resting on my shoulder, yelling at children to get off my lawn.

I laughed a little at the thought, then stopped as soon as I strolled into Elysium Central. The common space held two things: the Central Market, and the Elders' castle.

Since Elysium Central was the only neutral space on the

island, the Central Market was where people from all territories set up shop to sell their wares and services. Some had permanent shops, others could be found in temporary structures that cropped up on an as-needed basis.

But while the shops might change, one thing about the Central Market had always been true, throughout the entirety of my childhood: it was busy. Loud. Bustling.

What I walked through now felt like a ghost town. There were none of the temporary vendor stalls that should have been crowding the space, and all of the permanent establishments were quiet, like strolling down the main street of a ghost town. If the businesses were open, if anyone was inside them, it didn't show.

I almost stopped and waited for Luca and Gareth to catch up, so I could ask them what the hell was going on. But in the end I reminded myself that I didn't care, and I forged on ahead to the castle.

The castle really *was* a castle, something that had never seemed weird to me until I went to the mortal world, and castles were medieval structures feudal lords lived in. Then again, on second thought, it really wasn't that weird. Every country's seat of power housed itself in some sort of excessively-large, imposing building. The Elysium Elders had simply gone with the castle architecture.

It did have a disappointing lack of a moat, and frankly, from a defensive standpoint, it lacked the advantages a castle was supposed to have. It wasn't on high ground and it didn't even have an outer wall. Of course, in the history of Elysium, no one had ever, to my knowledge, challenged the Elders' rule.

The six men and women who governed Elysium were the only true immortals on the island. Where their longevity came from, I didn't know. Rumor claimed that when Elysium was born, the Elders forged a link to the wellspring of its magic, and it was that connection that kept them from aging.

The rest of us weren't like that. For all we referred to the world outside of Elysium as "the mortal realm," Elysians didn't live forever. Our lifespans were longer than most, averaging somewhere between one-hundred and one-hundred-and-fifty years, but we did die.

The island would be crazy over-populated, otherwise, even given that it was a magical island that tended to expand as needed to house its current population. Despite that, we didn't tend to breed at uncontrollable rates since Elysian magic allowed women to choose if and when we got pregnant. Men had the same choice—it took both partners being on board, so to speak, for an Elysian couple to conceive.

If there was one thing that horrified me the most about the mortal world, it was the lack of choice over conception. I hadn't been sure if my magic would handle that part of my life in Arizona, and I had used the hell out of condoms as a result.

I approached the castle doors and saw the two customary guards to either side today were two members of the Icarii, the winged people that claimed territory on the northeastern side of the island and made their homes in the cliff-sides there. They both had wings of a deep auburn that shone with gold, reaching six inches above their head at the wings' peaks, the bottom feathers an inch above the ground.

They were also barring my way. The moment I'd come within five feet of them they'd crossed the spears they held, blocking the doorway.

I waved a hand in front of me. "Destined one, here. I get dragged back from the mortal realm and this is the kind of welcome I get?"

They ignored me, gazes going over my shoulders to where Luca and Gareth approached behind me.

"Ashlynn Hunter is here to see the Elders," Luca said.

I withheld an audible snort. Sure, that would work. They hadn't believed *me,* but—

It worked. The guards, still silent—was that a new requirement?—lifted their spears, bowed, and stepped aside.

"Seriously? You needed a man to confirm it for you?"

The guards still didn't speak, but the one on the right's lips twitched, as if he was perilously close to laughing and desperately trying not to.

"Don't take it personally," Luca murmured as we stepped through the doors, "there have been reports of the Darkness taking human likeness. Without your Heartstone, you're impossible to verify as human, much less Elysian."

I would have said something about proving my Hunter strength by bashing their heads together, but I was too busy staring. I'd never actually been inside the Elders' castle before. When I was a kid, the public spaces of the castle had been open to anyone, with guards placed only at the private quarters and meeting rooms, but I'd never had any interest in going. The only things I'd been interested in before I left were new weapons and running wild with Luca.

My chest twinged. I dug the heel of my palm into it, trying to soothe a hurt I wasn't certain was physical.

The castle's antechamber opened onto a floor of black and white tile like a chessboard, the walls covered in carved reliefs and painted scenes from Elysium's mythology, most of it to do with the island's origins. According to the legend, the sisters of Light and Darkness had created the world in harmony, and they had been worshipped as goddesses in tandem.

As time went on, man grew to favor the Light, and the Darkness grew jealous of her sister. The two fought, and to keep the Darkness from destroying the world they had built, the Light locked the Darkness away beneath the Star of

Elysium. To power the prison, the Light sank herself into the island. From her power the Elysians were born, the Heart-stones her gift to her children, each Elysian life and death a reincarnation of the Light itself, a cycle that powered the Star and kept the Darkness at bay.

Frankly, I'd always thought of it as an over-simplified bedtime story: don't step out of line, or you'll set the Darkness free. But everyone had believed the Oracle when he'd said Elysium's failing crops and sudden increase in sickness was the Darkness returning to the world. Everyone believed him when he said it was because I, and the other five girls who'd been banished, had torn too much power from Elysium. We'd gone from being the island's pride to the cause of all its problems.

"Are you all right?" Luca asked.

I realized I'd stopped in the middle of the antechamber, staring at the floor-to-ceiling statues of the Light and her sister the Darkness. The statues were actually a fountain, their eyes weeping water into a basin that was half white, half black, the opposite color beneath each statue. I found it disturbing.

And I didn't like the myth. If the mortal world had taught me anything, it was that history was written by the victors, and nothing was truly black and white.

"Ash?"

I tore my gaze away from the fountain.

"I'm fine. I don't know where I'm going." Luca gave me a strange look and I realized my hand was still clasped over my chest like I was having a heart attack. I lowered it to my side.

"This way."

I started to follow Luca but stopped when I realized Gareth wasn't doing the same.

"I'm afraid this is as far as I go," he said. "Elder business really isn't to my taste."

"Coward," I accused.

Gareth swept me a little bow. "Guilty as charged. Have fun."

I rolled my eyes and followed Luca out of the antechamber, through the double doors that rested between two staircases. They swung open silently without Luca's aid, as if some ghostly attendant had seen our approach and waved them open.

The floor ceased its checkered pattern inside the room we walked into, discarding black in favor of a blinding white that would have hurt my eyes if the room's lighting hadn't been so dim. It was a fully interior room, no windows, the only apparent source of light filtering down from a small round skylight that cast a murky beam of sun into a four-foot diameter circle in the center of the room.

Six chairs—thrones would be more accurate, given their size and the intricacy of the carvings that covered them—surrounded that patch of light, each one set equidistance apart from the others. They were empty, but Luca led us to stand directly in the circle of light anyway.

At least, *he* stepped into it. I stayed firmly outside of the circle of both light and thrones. I didn't care for the power play inherent in the fact that if I stepped into that circle and the Elders decided to grace us with their presence and take their seats, it would be impossible not to have at least two of them at my unguarded back.

I had been intently avoiding thoughts of seeing the Elders, of speaking to them. Now that I was in this room, the hairs on the back of my neck were stiff, my palms had gone sweaty, and the pain in my chest was now a remembered one.

The day they had banished us, each Elder took one of us on a boat into the ocean and dropped anchor right before the boundary. It was the only time I'd seen an Elder, and I could still remember her face. Young, and smooth, her skin as white as alabaster, making mine look twice as dark for her paleness. She'd had all the expression, all the empathy, of stone, too.

She'd offered me the choice of removing my Heartstone, or having it removed. If I'd done it myself, it wouldn't have hurt. It is no pain to touch your own heart, after all. But I hadn't wanted to make it easy for her. When I'd told her *no*, she'd smiled. It hadn't been a pretty smile.

I could still feel her fingers against my chest, nails scraping flesh, the pain as she grasped the edges of my Heartstone and ripped it free. The agony had been excruciating. Enough so that I'd passed out, and I didn't actually remember my journey through the boundary.

"Ash." Luca held out his hand.

I found my voice, somehow. "No, thank you. I'm not stepping into the creepy light circle."

"The Elders won't come in until you do."

"Then I guess the Elders won't be talking to me." Which was absolutely fine because I had no desire to talk to them. They'd wanted me to show up here, I'd shown up. If they weren't going to talk to me because I wouldn't step into their circle, that was *their* problem.

I turned, intent on marching back out the way I'd come. The massive double doors swung shut at the behest of their invisible operator. I was firmly of the belief that no doors that large and that heavy should be able to move without making a single sound.

I walked up to them. They bore no handle to grasp, so I searched the walls for a lever or mechanism of some kind, but found nothing. I tried shoving on them, even though they'd opened inward, but I might as well have been a bee hurling myself at a solid stone wall for all they budged.

I kept trying, ignoring the panic that clawed at the back of my throat. I broke my fingernails scrabbling at the door, trying to gain some purchase with which to haul them open.

Hands closed over mine, held them still. I was breathing too hard, too fast.

"It'll be all right, Ash." Luca's hand reached up to brush my hair out of my face and I jerked away from the touch. I didn't need his pity, and I didn't want it either.

His lips pressed into a thin line. "They're not going to let us out until we talk to them, and they're not going to talk to us until we get in the damn circle."

"Fine." I wished I could say I sounded pissed, but I barely managed the word as more than a whisper. "But you'd better have my back, Luca Ferrar. Because if you don't, I'll put a dagger in yours."

17

LUCA

Ashlynn was terrified, and I cursed myself for not realizing sooner that that would be her reaction. I didn't know what had happened between her and the Elder who'd overseen her exile, but one didn't get a Heartstone scar by giving it away willingly. And Ashlynn had never given anything away willingly.

Thinking of that moment, when they must have ripped it from her, made the wolf rise inside me, claws sheathing the tips of my fingers. I fought the change because it wouldn't do me any good here, and because I needed to be able to talk for Ashlynn's sake.

But the wolf did not go willingly, and that alone told me how close my other half was to considering myself mated, cemented bond or no. I'd told myself when I went to get her that I could keep things neutral. Friendly. I'd known she wouldn't want me and I'd convinced myself I would think of her with affection, like she was a little sister, and nothing more.

I'd been an idiot. There was absolutely nothing familial about my feelings for her. Hadn't been since the moment I'd seen her at that bar. If I wasn't very, very careful, I was going to start treating her like she was mine. And if I did that—if I did that, I'd lose her.

"Are we doing this or not?" Ash snapped. The harsher she spoke, the more bravado she put into it, the more nervous she was.

"Yeah." I stepped into the circle. She came with me and put her back to mine, like we were two fighters in the middle of a sea of enemies. Which was probably how she viewed it.

When the Elders appeared, she jumped—not enough to be visible, just enough for me to feel the slight hitch where her back met mine—and I couldn't blame her. It was creepy as hell when they all simply appeared, thrones empty one second, occupied the next. I'd at least seen it before. Ash hadn't.

The Elders, though present, did not see fit to speak immediately. They stared at Ashlynn instead. *Appraised* was a better word for the way they looked at her, and it had claws shredding the skin at my fingertips again.

Only three of the Elders could see her given our positions, my back to hers, and once those had stared their fill the thrones shifted in tandem, as if they sat on a ring and someone had spun it so that the other three came to rest in front of her. I heard her swallow, felt her fingers clench into fists, and I knew that whichever Elder had taken her Heartstone faced her now.

I wanted to take her hand, to reassure her, but I didn't know what the Elders would do if she rejected me in front of them. When it seemed like the silence would stretch on forever, the Elder in front of me, Ansarus, finally spoke.

"Did you have difficulty retrieving her, Luca Ferrar?"

Before I could answer, in as diplomatic way as I could manage, that Ashlynn was not a thing to be fetched, she did it for me. In as *un*diplomatic a way as possible.

"I wasn't *retrieved*. I chose to come back, and if I don't like what I hear, I'm taking myself back to the mortal realm."

"You may certainly try," a smooth, silk voice answered. Shiernan. No other Elder had a voice that poisonously pretty. "But the border was only unsealed long enough to allow you to be found and returned. You will find it is unwilling to grant you passage."

I could feel Ashlynn's fury, knew it was directed at me. I hadn't known she wouldn't be able to leave again once we came here, but I doubted that would matter much to her, even if she did believe me. I was surprised she didn't immediately argue with them, but I understood why a moment later when she said, "The others. I want to see them."

"As do we all," Shiernan replied. "But alas, you are the first of the Six to return to us."

"What do you want from me?"

"For now? We only wished to verify your presence. The prophecy the Oracle spoke shall not come to pass until the six of you are present together in Elysium, once more."

"That's *it*?" Ash said. I'd never heard a person put that much incredulity into two words. "You ripped out my Heartstone and threw me out of my home on a prophecy's whim. Now you've brought me back on one, and you want me to do nothing but *wait*?"

"Yes," Shiernan replied with infuriating calm.

This was precisely what I'd been afraid of. The Darkness grew bolder, stronger, by the day and the Elders did nothing. Though we couldn't kill the Darkness on our own, we *could* diminish its presence in Elysium by fighting it, but the Elders refused to order even that much resistance. But if I showed them that Ashlynn could *destroy* the Dark, maybe they would listen.

"Elders," I said inclining my head in deference. "If I may, Ashlynn has fought the Darkness and—"

"You were under strict orders not to bring her into contact with the Darkness," Ansarus hissed.

"And I did not do so intentionally. The Darkness attacked us in the mortal realm. In shadow. And though it may have been dangerous, it was an unexpected gift."

"In what way?" This from Endarian, the Elder seated to Ansarus' right.

"She killed a Slither." I reached into the bag, pulled out the Slither's body and decapitated head, and laid them on the floor at Endarian's feet, just inside the light circle. He shifted forward slightly to look more closely, which was the most I'd ever seen an Elder move here in this room. They tended to sit like statues, only the movement of their mouths a testament to the fact they were alive.

"Intriguing," Endarian said, in a tone that implied the opposite. "Though it should come as no real surprise that one of the prophesied should have an effect on the Darkness that we ourselves cannot. This is merely a confirmation of what the Oracle has promised."

I tried and failed to control my frustration. "Surely now is the time to fight back in earnest. If we can understand how Ashlynn is able to kill the Darkness, instead of merely dissipate it, we can improve safety. We can—"

"We will not risk the prophecy by intentionally putting Ashlynn in the Darkness' path," Ilorna broke in. She was Endarian's twin, their features both identical and androgynous, so that it was nearly impossible to tell them apart until one spoke.

"People are dying," I said. Who knew how long it would take the other five to return to Elysium? I had found Ashlynn quickly, but I had a werewolf's nose. How long would it take for the others' mates to find them? How much longer to convince them to return? We needed to act now. "People have *been* dying and they are going to keep dying until we put a stop to it."

"Then they will continue to die." This was Torrival's voice, spoken from behind me, cold and unyielding. "Better that a few should die now, than the prophecy should fail and Elysium should perish. Understand our will on this, Luca Ferrar. You will not take Ashlynn to fight the Darkness. Is this understood?"

"Yes," I ground out. Torrival had left me a sizable loophole in that understanding and I intended to exploit it.

"Good. Now—"

Ashlynn cut him off. "Let me get this straight. You don't want me to fight. You don't, in fact, want me to do anything at all, except sit around and wait for the others to show up? What do you think is going to happen? We're going to sit in the same room together and the Darkness is magically going to vanish?"

"You forget your place, girl," Heskala, silent until now, broke in. "You are returned to Elysium by *our* grace, and you will—"

"You act as if I did something to deserve being thrown out in the first place," Ash cut in. I could only conclude she was trying to find out if suicide by Elders was a viable path to death. "What was my crime again? When I was *twelve?*"

I didn't expect anyone to answer that. I don't think Ash did either. But Endarian did.

"The Heartstones draw their power from Elysium itself. The six of you took too much from the island."

"Seriously? Being born? That's the crime you're going with? Maybe you should have blamed our parents for that."

"View it as an injustice if you so choose," Ilorna said, as if it didn't matter much to her either way. Then again, it probably didn't. "But what was done was done for the greater good. As you are here now for the greater good. Your displeasure with this fact will change nothing."

I could hear Ash grit her teeth. "And my Heartstone? Where is it?"

"We attempted to return them to the island," Ansarus said. There was the briefest hesitation before he'd spoken, and I was struck with the absolute certainty that he was lying, which he continued right on doing. "But Elysium would not reclaim them, or their power. We now understand, of course, that this was because you were meant to return and reclaim them yourselves."

"Wonderful," Ash said, her voice laden with sarcasm. "I'm here to reclaim."

"You understand what is required of you if you desire the return of that stone," Ansarus replied, but the reply was spoken more to me, and it held the hint of a question. I tensed.

"No," Ash said, "I don't."

Ansarus lifted an eyebrow at me, and I gave the slightest shake of my head.

"Ah. I am certain it will come to you in time. Suffice it to say that your Heartstone will be returned to you once you have earned it."

"But I—"

"That is all for now, Ashlynn Hunter. You may leave. Luca Ferrar—you will stay."

I thought Ash might argue again, but in the end she simply moved for the space between two Elders. I grabbed her wrist. "Wait for me," I said softly. "Please."

She shrugged. I took it for all the assent I was going to get and let her go.

18

ASHLYNN

I held my breath as I passed through the space between two of the Elders' thrones. They reminded me, in both appearance and mannerisms, of nothing so much as the mortal legends of vampires.

It occurred to me that maybe those legends weren't unreasonable. Mortal myths about werewolves were true, after all, and if those legends had come from Elysium... The Elders *had* been around for, well, *ever*.

I could certainly see Shiernan drinking someone's blood. It had taken everything I had to stand in front of her, to look into her eyes when my skin was feeling her fingers ripping my Heartstone from me. As unhappy as I currently was with Luca, if he hadn't been at my back no force in this world would have kept me in that circle.

As it was, now that I was *out*, the solid black doors slamming shut behind me, I wasn't going to stick around. Luca had asked me to, but I hadn't promised I would. If he was so used to people doing what he asked that he assumed I'd comply, well, that was *his* problem.

When I stormed past the fountain of the Light and the Darkness, Gareth shoved off the wall he'd been holding up and scrambled after me. He looked like he'd been bored senseless. Given that he was the only person in the room, I imagined he had been.

And wasn't it odd that he was the only person in the room? That the entire Elders' castle seemed deserted save for the two guards out front? I may not have wandered into the structure itself in my youth, but I'd passed it plenty. People had always been going in and out of it. I remembered vaguely that it was purported to hold an art gallery, where various Elysians competed to have their works displayed, and a number of other public rooms for meetings and social gatherings.

Not to mention the leaders of each territory met regularly with the Elders to discuss the inevitable squabbles that came up when multiple factions lived on one island and the only option for leaving was going to the mortal world. There had been a lot of meetings.

So where the hell was everyone now?

I shoved the doors open to the outside, hoping but failing to startle the two Icarii guards. I was ten feet past them before Gareth put on a burst of speed and jumped in front of me.

"Hey, where are you going?"

"Away."

"Where's Luca?"

"The Elders wanted to talk to him some more. You should probably wait for him."

Gareth looked uncomfortable. "You probably shouldn't go off on your own."

"Are you suggesting I can't take care of myself, Gareth?" I put every ounce of warning and menace I had into the question, wolf style. Suggesting a wolf couldn't take care of herself was one of the greatest offenses a pack member could give, and if I wasn't technically a pack member, I'd once held honorary status.

"Hey, easy, Ash, I'm not suggesting anything like that."

"Good. Then there's no issue with me going."

Gareth still didn't move out of my way and he looked, if possible, more uncomfortable. "Luca won't like it."

"Luca can go stick his head in quicksand for all I care. He's not *my* pack prince. I don't have to do what he says. So unless there's some explanation you could give me for why it's so vitally important I wait here for him like a good little pup...?"

Gareth swallowed.

That's right. Go ahead. Tell me I'm supposed to be the Hunter/White Woods pack sacrificial bride.

"No explanation I can give you, no."

So Luca had sworn him to secrecy then. "Pack prince got your tongue?" I said, sweetly enough to cause a host of instant cavities.

"Come on, Ash, cut me a break."

"Nope. Not my problem. I'm going. You're staying. Follow me and I will get violent. Clear?"

"He's gonna kill me."

"Now you're just being dramatic," I said. "Unless Luca's turned into a completely different person in the last few years, the most you'll suffer is some bruises. Maybe a short-lived bone fracture or two. You'll heal in half an hour."

I turned away before Gareth's puppy dog eyes could guilt me into either staying or letting him tag along. I broke into a lope and headed for the Hunter territory.

I didn't want to see my father again. But if what Luca had said was true, if he was dying—I swallowed hard and increased my pace, trying to focus on the pleasant burn that developed in my legs and not the fact that I was going home.

I'd loved my father. My mom had died when I was six, and Luca and my father had been everything to me. Until they weren't. Until the Oracle's prophecy, when Luca let me go, and my father lost all affection for me in the blink of an eye.

I would give Dad the chance, just the one, to apologize.

❧ 19 ❧

LUCA

"WHY HAVE YOU NOT TOLD HER OF THE PROPHECY'S requirement?" Ansarus asked. He was, in my limited experience with the Elders, the most human-seeming of them. I wasn't certain that that didn't make him the most dangerous one. "Her Heartstone must be joined with yours. You understood this when we entrusted it to your care."

"I can't make her love me on sight. It's going to take time."

"She need not love you," Shiernan said. "Love is not required to meld a Heartstone—only her willingness."

I raised an eyebrow in incredulity. "You heard how willing she is with regards to prophecy. She has no intention of doing anything you want. If I tell her about the Heartstone, she'll dig her heels in for the simple pleasure of refusing you."

Shiernan sniffed. "I *did* feel such obstinacy when I tore it from her all those years ago."

My hands clenched into fists.

"Careful, wolf," Shiernan purred. "You wouldn't want us to take you as a threat, would you?"

I uncurled my fingers and flexed them.

"Better," Shiernan said. "I am sure we can attribute it to soon-to-be-mated werewolf territoriality. As for Ashlynn, if you believe convincing her she loves you is the necessary path, you may yet have enough time for that. But Luca?

"Willingness is a slippery thing. The only thing the girl need do, as far as we are concerned, is break her Heartstone herself. If you cannot make her do it out of love, we will encourage her to do it by *other* means. See it is done before the other five return. That is all."

The Elders disappeared, there one blink, gone the next. I didn't let my anger show. I didn't know where they went when they vanished, or how they did it, but I wasn't convinced they couldn't observe everything in this room whether they appeared to be in it or not. I didn't want them to change their minds about taking the choice away from Ash.

Guilt nipped at the edges of my conscience. I didn't *like* lying to her. Maybe I could have told her the truth, if she hadn't been so *Ashlynn* when I found her. If the anger and fierce protectiveness that hovered just beneath my skin *wasn't* soon-to-be-mated werewolf territoriality.

I wanted Ashlynn. I wanted her desperately, and I didn't want to throw away the possibility of a future with her. And if I told her what was happening, what the Elders wanted, that's exactly what I would be doing. Because Ashlynn would never submit. She would never agree to be mine if she knew it was precisely what the Elders wanted.

But the guilt wouldn't leave me alone. If I managed to keep it from her, if she did by some miracle come to love me, did I honestly think I had a chance in hell of keeping this from her forever? And if she found out after she'd split her Heartstone, after she'd given half to me, I would be bound for all eternity to a woman who hated my guts.

There had to be a way to give the Elders what they wanted and not lose her. I just didn't know what the hell it was yet.

The massive doors swung open. I took a deep breath and schooled my face into neutrality, trying to hide my conflicted thoughts. I certainly didn't need Ash seeing them before I figured out what to do. It turned out not to be an issue, because Ashlynn wasn't there when I walked out. Only Gareth was, pacing back and forth in front of the fountain.

Maybe she was just waiting outside. Except if she was waiting outside, Gareth should be with her. His head jerked up, met my gaze, and I knew from the way his jaw clenched she was gone. Damn it, I'd *asked* her to wait.

"Where is she?"

"She took off toward Hunter territory."

A trickle of fear settled into my chest, one I had no solid basis for. Elysium should be safe enough in the daylight hours. She was the damn heir to Hunter, she could take care of herself, and she was prophecy-named. No one in Elysium should harm her. But no matter how I told myself that, the raw knot of worry wouldn't stop building.

"Then why they hell aren't you with her?"

"I tried to go with her. She refused. Have you ever tried to do something she doesn't want you to do? Short of getting in a physical altercation with her, which goes against my principles and which she would probably lay me out flat for since I don't actually want to hurt her, I didn't have much of a choice.

"She might have let me tag along if I could have told her *why* you don't want her going off alone, but as she so succinctly put it, the pack prince has my mouth sealed shut."

I refrained from punching my best friend in the face. Both because he was my best friend, and because he was right. I stormed past him, out the doors of the Elders' castle.

"Where are you going?" Gareth asked, trotting after me.

"To retrieve her," I growled.

20

ASHLYNN

THE HUNTER TERRITORY HADN'T CHANGED IN MY ABSENCE. It was as if the whole place was a postcard stamped in my memory, frozen in time, waiting for me to come back before it started moving again. Baerlin and Sarena, the territory's two resident blacksmiths, still kept shop at the outskirts, where the heat and noise of their work wouldn't bother any of the inhabitants.

I paused for a moment to watch them, Sarena hammering out the blade of a sword, Baerlin pouring molten metal for arrow tips into a mould. Their shops were opposite each other, at the head of the path that led into Hunter territory proper, but the only rivalry between them was friendly. Their specialties differed, and both were happy playing to their strengths and sending customers to the other when it made the most sense.

When I was a kid, I could watch them for hours—*had* watched them for hours. I had wanted to apprentice to Sarena, though when I'd announced as much to Dad, he'd flat out told me the Hunter heir didn't do that kind of work. I was supposed to be a symbol. I was supposed to work hard to be the best Hunter, the best fighter.

Power, he'd told me, was kept by staying above the menial, not embracing it. The speech hadn't sat well with me when I was a kid, though I hadn't understood why. I'd just admired the skill it took to craft a blade. Now, I recognized the words for the keep-the-status-quo, authoritarian bullshit they were.

If either Baerlin or Sarena noticed me, they didn't acknowledge it, and after a while I admitted I was stalling and I set off down the path, into the heart of Hunter territory. It was an organic settlement, groups of houses ringed around the necessities of Hunter life: sparring rings and archery fields, obstacle courses and training houses.

No one paid me any mind as I walked through. My features weren't that distinct from any other Hunter's, nothing about me that would scream Barren's daughter to people who hadn't seen me since I was a child. A far different experience from my youth, when everyone had been only too eager to be my friend.

I'd simply thought people liked me, then. I hadn't really questioned that if I wanted a friend, I had one. If I wanted something, it was given to me. If I had an idea, it was well-received. It had taken meeting Luca, and more than one snide comment from him, for me to understand that people hadn't liked me. They hadn't necessarily *dis*liked me, they just hadn't been seeing me at all. I had been a figurehead and a means to an end. I was the heir to Hunter, and getting in my good graces had meant potential gain immediately if I reported nice things to my father, or later when I one day took control of the territory myself.

Once I'd understood that, I'd started spending almost all of my time with the wolves. So much so that, after my own people realized I was no longer an easy inroad to my father's good graces, I'd been on the receiving end of more than a few rude comments about throwing over my own kind for our "barbaric" neighbors.

I arrived at my childhood home too soon. My feet had carried me there on autopilot while my mind had lost itself in memory. The house itself was as I remembered it. Set on the opposite side of the settlement I'd entered from, it was built practically into the beachside cliffs, leaving only two sides that needed defending in the event of an attack.

That such an attack would only ever come from within the Hunter territory was something I hadn't thought to be bitter about until I'd spent time in the mortal realm. For all that the six Elysian territories verbally sparred with one another, as far as I knew, there had never been a war within Elysium's borders. Maybe it was because we lived on an island, and people understood the bloodbath feuding with one's neighbors in a finite space would be, but I doubted it.

Individual people might be that level-headed, but most weren't, and considering each group on this damn island had a clearly-defined identity they thought set them apart from and elevated them above their neighbors, the six territories tended to have tempers flaring more often than not. I attributed lack of actual war to the Elders' influence, and though I didn't understand it, it was the one good thing I considered them to have done.

All of which was to say, the defensible nature of my childhood home was meant as a bulwark against anyone *within* the Hunter territory deciding that maybe they could lead better than the lineage that bore our territory's name. Which really begged the question, if my father was sick, why hadn't anyone killed him yet?

The answer to that question presented itself—or, rather, *himself*—when I forced myself to knock on the door. At something over six feet, with the dark brown hair and tanned skin that was almost a guarantee if one was Hunter-born, the man who opened the door to my father's house was the embodiment of all things Hunter: impressive, muscled physique, I-will-eat-you-for-breakfast stare, and a singular lack of weaponry anywhere on him that told me he thought a great deal of himself.

He didn't utter a single word in greeting, merely lifted an eyebrow in a manner that condescendingly demanded to know who I was and why the fuck I was interrupting his day. I knew that eyebrow lift, that haughty demeanor. I had both of them, and they'd been drilled into me by my father. Looked like Barren Hunter had plucked someone from the Hunter territory to take my place as heir once he let me get chucked off the island.

"I'm here to see Barren," I said.

The man looked, of all things, resigned. "Fine." But he didn't let me in. He stepped outside and shut the door behind him. "Let's get this over with before my lunch gets cold."

I connected the dots a second before his fist flew at my face. He thought I was here to challenge Barren for leadership of Hunter, and he was fighting as my father's proxy. What would you know, somebody cared enough about the old asshole to fight his battles for him when he was down. I supposed I shouldn't be surprised—I'd have done the same thing before Dad tossed me aside like trash.

I ducked the strike and pivoted, opened my mouth to tell him that I wasn't here in challenge. But the familiar zing of adrenaline hit me, joy singing in my veins as I recognized a worthy opponent, and I shut my mouth. I *wanted* this fight, and I gave myself over to it, to the familiar dance of strike and dodge, strike and block.

Whoever the man was, he was good—Barren Hunter wouldn't waste the time training anyone who wasn't. If I cared to admit it—which I didn't—he would probably beat me in a fair fight. I had trained in the mortal realm, because it was in my blood to do so and I couldn't stop, but I'd had a dearth of instructive knowledge. As a kid, I'd been left with whatever free martial arts programs I could find, and as an adult I hadn't been able to afford much better. Add in that martial arts sparring held very little in common with an actual fight, where the goal was to either hurt, disable, or kill, and I was at a distinct disadvantage.

But I had one thing going for me that this man didn't. He was clearly accustomed to winning. I would wager the clothes on my back—which were currently my only possession—that he hadn't lost a fight in a very long time. He knew his technique was better and he'd accepted his victory as a foregone conclusion. The only reason I wasn't already on my ass was that I was just a hair faster than him, and I'd so far managed to keep him from turning this into a grappling match.

I reconsidered that last thought when I landed a couple of punches of my own. I was so used to how my body functioned in the mortal world that I'd forgotten just how much strength had flooded into me on my return. Strength that nearly cracked ribs when my second punch landed.

He grunted and surprise and confusion flashed across his face for the briefest moment before he hid it. I couldn't stop the grin that took over my face. Didn't even want to. I was *stronger* than him.

He'd figured it out, too, if the way he picked up speed and launched a flurry of attacks that sent me into a defensive spiral was any indication. He'd just realized there was a possibility, however slim, that he might not win this, and he'd decided to stop fucking around.

I took a couple hits I could have dodged, let myself falter a couple times when I wasn't really tired. Then I gave him an opening, not so obvious he'd know it was a trap, and he lunged for it. I sidestepped and grabbed his wrist as he flew past me, pulled his arm behind his back and up, locking it in place. At the same time, I took out his legs and drove him to the ground, my knee in his lower back pinning him there.

I might be stronger, but he had at least sixty pounds on me, and when he bucked beneath me, trying to flip our positions, I almost lost him. Even the extra torque I put on his arm didn't quell his efforts entirely. Time to stop playing. I pulled my knife and pressed the sharp tip to where the base of his skull met his spinal column.

He went still instantly. There were two rules about a challenge to Hunter leadership. One, the fight was to the death. Two, weapons weren't allowed.

"If you have to cheat to lead the territory," he spat, "you'll never hold on to it."

I sighed. "Fun though this has been—" and it *had* been fun "—this is the part where I tell you there's been a big misunderstanding. I have no interest in leading Hunter. In fact, I'm rather glad that you, whoever the fuck you are, have taken the irritating necessity off my hands in my absence.

"But to clarify things, when I said I was here to see Barren, I meant I was here to see my *father*."

If I thought the man beneath me had gone still when I pressed the knife to him, he went more so now, as if sinking into an immobility so complete that it embodied the very ideal of stillness.

"Ashlynn?"

No shit.

"Luca actually found you?"

I could hear the disbelief—and the bitterness—in his voice. Poor little Hunter thought I was here to steal his throne. Had he missed the part where I said I didn't want it?

"Yes, the big bad wolf dragged me home. Everyone's happy except me. And you, apparently. By the way, who *are* you?"

"Get off me and I'll tell you."

"Are you going to try to kill me again?"

He thought about it for a good two seconds before he said, grudgingly, "No."

I let him go. He rolled to his feet, his gaze sweeping over me. "How do I know it's really you?"

Seriously? Who the fuck would want *to be me right now?* Then I remembered there were a lot of idiots in the world. "You know anyone *else* in Elysium missing her Heartstone?" I pulled aside the V-neck collar of my shirt to reveal the jagged scar over my chest.

His eyes widened and a hint of a smirk graced his lips. "Nice tattoo."

I released my shirt collar, covering up Luca's name. Fuck that fucking tattoo. It had seemed like a good idea at the time. Then again, at the time, I'd been drunk off my ass and one-hundred percent positive I was never going to see Luca Ferrar again.

"Mention it to anyone and I will personally come back here and kill your ass."

"He hasn't seen it yet, then? Where is he, anyway? I'm surprised he let you out of his sight."

"He's not my fucking keeper, and we're not talking about me anymore. We're talking about you. Who are *you*?"

The glint of amusement in his eyes vanished. "Devryn Ryder."

I should have guessed. The blue eyes were a near-giveaway. Almost everyone in the Hunter territory had brown eyes. It wasn't unheard of for us to have children with someone outside of our group—inbreeding would become a serious problem if we didn't—but most people stuck within our boundaries. As such, blue eyes were still a rarity among us, and I didn't remember anyone else in our age range who had them.

Devryn had been a couple years older than me and his

situation…I almost couldn't look him in the eye as the shame bit into me. His mother had been an unrepentant alcoholic, and no one had any idea who his father was. His mother had claimed she didn't know either, and I don't think anyone bothered to try and find out.

Marlena Ryder had been considered a stain on the Hunter legacy, which was pretty hypocritical, all things considered. It wasn't as if she was the only alcoholic in the history of Hunters. No, it was just that she was a female alcoholic, and she didn't bother to hide it.

But I wasn't feeling shame because of her. It was because, instead of helping Devryn, the Hunter community had collectively turned its back on him. As if his mother's failings were ones he deserved to pay for. He'd been a shunned, underfed kid and no one had lifted a finger to help him. Myself included.

I could rationalize my actions, claim I'd been a kid and I hadn't really understood what was happening, and that was true, up to a point. Once I'd met Luca, I hadn't spent much time in Hunter lands, eager to escape all the sycophants hoping to gain favor with my father. But I *had* seen Devryn. And the last couple years I'd spent in Elysium, I'd been old enough to start understanding things. Of all the fucking people in Hunter territory, if *I'd* defended Devryn, people would have been forced to accept him. To at least not turn a blind eye to the fact his mom never had money for food.

But I hadn't done a damn thing. Some people are inherently good, as if they're born with some moral compass that unerringly points to true north. But I hadn't been like that. I hadn't been a *bad* person. It wasn't as if I'd spent my spare time picking on the less fortunate and torturing puppies. But I hadn't really given a thought to anyone but myself. And Luca.

Not until I got tossed out into a world I didn't understand, all my status and privilege ripped away, and I discovered how the other shoe fit. Discovered exactly what it was like to be the person no one wanted, that everyone wished would just grow up and go away, so they didn't have to deal with me anymore.

Irony of all ironies, Devryn and I had switched places in life. It was an absolutely brilliant move on my father's part. If he hadn't chosen an heir to replace me, everyone in the Hunter territory would have been trying to weasel their way into being chosen. And Devryn would have been the perfect choice. Still young, still malleable, and absolutely desperate.

Barren Hunter wouldn't have had to offer Devryn much more than food and a roof that wasn't his mother's and the kid would have been his. Clearly *was* his, if Devryn was defending Barren when all he had to do to claim leadership of the Hunters was challenge the man while he was weak.

"Are you going to stare at me all day," Devryn asked, making me realize I had indeed been staring for several seconds, "or did you want to see your father?"

"Am I welcome in the house?"

Devryn shrugged. "Couldn't say. He hasn't been lucid for days."

He walked up to the front door and opened it before I found my tongue again. "What exactly is wrong with him?"

Devryn glanced back at me, sharply. "Luca didn't tell you?"

"There wasn't really time to go into details," I lied. I hadn't asked, because I hadn't really wanted to know. I'd been more interested in fucking Luca in the shower than talking about dear old Dad. Because I'd been pissed at Dad. Was *still* pissed at him. The fact that he was sick didn't alter what he'd done to me.

"He's Darksick," Devryn said, quietly, as I followed him inside.

I didn't ask him what the Darksickness *was*, what it did.

Not yet. I wanted to see Barren Hunter for myself, first. *Then* I'd demand answers.

My first thought on walking in was that the house hadn't changed at all. Same furniture, same arrangement, same layout. My second thought was that it *had* changed, but the changes were so subtle, I'd missed them at first. Anywhere that something of *me* had existed—the rug I'd bought my father for his birthday one year, the painting of me and my father that used to hang above the mantelpiece—the item in question had been replaced.

The round gray rug I'd bought him was now a rectangular dark green one. And the painting above the mantel...well, there was one *there*. But it wasn't me standing in front of Barren with his hands on my shoulders. It was Devryn. He was so young in the painting my father must have had it commissioned within a year of my leaving. Devryn was skinny in it too, his cheeks still hollowed out with evidence of malnutrition.

It wasn't the only depiction of them, either. That was the centerpiece, but smaller paintings flanked it, Devryn older in each one.

"How soon?" I asked, my voice tight. I'd stopped walking, staring at the paintings. My hands had clenched into fists and I couldn't make them loosen.

"How soon for what?"

"How soon did he replace me?"

Devryn's jaw clenched, a muscle ticking along the side. He looked uncomfortable for the first time since he'd learned who I was. "Don't ask a question you don't want the answer to," he said finally.

"Six months?" I knew from the look on his face I was way off the mark. "One?" I asked softly. He still didn't answer. "Just fucking tell me."

"He came for me within the hour."

My knees wanted to give out but I refused to let them. I didn't have to ask *which* hour. In all likelihood, at the very moment Shiernan had been tearing out my Heartstone, my father had been calmly offering my place to Devryn. I'd thought—I'd thought my father loved me. His betrayal would have been easier if he'd been a terrible parent, but he hadn't. Not until the prophecy, anyway.

But within the *hour*? Barren Hunter wouldn't make a split-second decision about who to name as the Hunter heir. He valued the territory above all else. Which meant to come for Devryn so soon, my father had considered replacing me before I'd even left.

Devryn knew it as well as I did. There was something dangerously akin to pity in his dark blue eyes. I didn't want his pity. No doubt didn't want it any more than he wanted mine.

"That day—that wasn't the first time my father approached you, was it?"

"No."

"When?"

Devryn shrugged. "I was eleven. You would have been nine?"

"What did he say?"

"You really want to go through this?"

"Yes."

"Fine. He asked if I was interested in taking your place. Said he'd told you to make a choice, and you'd made the wrong one."

A sick feeling hollowed out in my stomach. My father and I had had our only real fight on my ninth birthday. He'd said I was spending too much time with the wolves. That I was becoming more wolf than Hunter, and it needed to end. That my place was here.

And I had told him, with all of a nine-year-old's indignation, that I could be just as much wolf as Hunter if I wanted to be. He'd looked at me for a long time, and then he'd just nodded, as if he'd gotten the answer to a question. He'd never brought it up again, and I'd just been grateful he wasn't going to force the issue and take away my best friend. He must have decided right then my loyalties were too split to remain the Hunter heir.

"Then what?" I asked. "He just let you starve for the next three years until I was out of the picture?"

"No," Devryn replied. "I *would* have starved if it hadn't been for him."

"Do you think he *cares* about you?"

"No. He was quite clear on that the first time he approached me. What he cares about is the continuance of the Hunter territory. The three years leading up to your banishment were a trial period for me, and I have no illusions I was the only one he approached.

"He made sure I didn't starve, and I worked my ass off to please him. Guess I did better than everyone else in the running."

"If you're so assured of your position, why does my being back make you nervous?"

"I'm not nervous."

Oh, but he was. "It's the fucking prophecy isn't it?" His silence was answer enough. He thought my being named one of the six saviors of Elysium might be enough to make my father revoke his decision and give the Hunter legacy back to me. As if I fucking wanted it.

"It doesn't matter," Devryn said, and his next words were spoken in the tone of a man trying to logically convince himself. "Barren will never accept a divide in your loyalties. If you're mated to Luca—"

"Why the fuck does everyone keep acting like Luca and I mating is a foregone conclusion?" I exploded. I could see

Aiden Ferrar wanting the match. But given what Devryn had told me about my father, I no longer thought he would have been pushing for the same union, even in the name of neighborly alliance.

"It's...not?"

"Why the hell *would* it be? And why is everyone so obsessed with my love life? Shouldn't you all be asking me how I plan to stop the bloody Darkness? But no. No one wants to talk about that. No one even wants to let me near the damn Darkness. Instead, everyone is obsessed with whether I am or am not fucking Luca. Why is that?"

The whole mess suddenly made very little sense, and I wanted an answer, some *reason* for all of this. And for the love of Elysium, if he told me it was because Luca and I had been joined at the hip as kids, I'd—

"The guy went nuts when the Elders banished you."

I snorted. "Sure. He went so nuts he was too much of a coward to even come say goodbye."

"It's hard to say goodbye when your dad has you locked in silver chains," Devryn said evenly.

My heart stuttered in my chest. "What?"

"He tried to convince the pack to keep the Elders from throwing you out. Aiden chained him to the Elder Tree. Way I heard it, Luca almost tore through his wrists trying to get free. They had to knock him out until you were gone and the borders were sealed.

"Aiden left him there for a full moon cycle for defying him."

A full moon cycle. I shuddered. Most of the mortals' beliefs about werewolves and the full moon were bullshit. But one thing was true. If they didn't shift at least once a month, they went absolutely berserk. Sometimes they got their sanity back, after. Sometimes they didn't. And if Luca had been chained in silver, it would have been impossible for him to shift.

"Why are you telling me this?" I asked.

"Self preservation. If you mate into the White Woods pack, Barren will never take you back." It was true. But I had a feeling it wasn't *all* of the truth, either. There was still something going on that no one was telling me. But even knowing that, even knowing that what Devryn had told me was meant to manipulate me, it couldn't change my reaction.

Luca hadn't abandoned me. My father had. My territory had. Elysium had. But Luca hadn't. In the mess that was my life, that was Elysium and this damn prophecy, I *did* have one thing: I had Luca. And he hadn't even tried to tell me. Probably because he'd known if he'd offered it, I wouldn't have believed him.

Suddenly, Luca living on the outskirts of the White Woods, his disdain for the pack, made sense. The Elder Tree was in the center of the White Woods, a lone, ancient sentinel in a clearing where all of the pack businesses were. And his father had chained him there. For weeks. Where everyone would see him.

I almost turned around and walked out right then. But I needed to understand something first. I pushed the door to my father's bedroom open and walked in. The first thing I noticed wasn't Barren Hunter lying on the bed, the covers tucked up to his chin. It wasn't even the deathly pallor of his face or the way his veins ran black beneath them.

It was the sick stagnancy of the air. The overwhelming sense of wrongness in the room. The entire space felt as if was filled with a suffocating miasma and I just couldn't smell it. I was certain the room *should* reek, only my nose wasn't picking anything up.

I didn't want to be in here, but I forced myself to stay, to walk to the bed. It was so tall the top mattress was at my chest level, and I had to climb onto the sideboard just to look at my dad. The blackness of the veins was even stranger on his face, the way they fanned like tiny spiderwebs beneath his eyes.

I held my hand in front of his face and snapped my fingers. He'd always been a light sleeper, but he didn't so much as twitch. Since I was plenty pissed, I slapped him. Nothing.

"He won't wake up." Devryn leaned against the doorjamb, carefully on the outside of the room.

"How did he get like this?"

"Isn't that what you're supposed to tell us?"

"According to the Elders, I'm supposed to wait quietly like a good little girl until the other five get brought back. Then our combined presence is going to magically cure the Darkness."

Devryn snorted. "You plan on doing what they say?"

I started to answer that it didn't matter to me one way or the other. That I *hadn't* come back here to solve Elysium's problems. And it was true. I hadn't. But seeing Devryn, remembering the kid he'd been, the *nothing* I'd done then, my snapped reply that I hadn't *asked* for any of this died before it ever left my lips.

I wasn't a kid anymore, but I was still approaching the problem here with all the anger and resentment I'd felt when I was. I was being just as self-centered, just as selfish, as I had then.

I had a right to be pissed. What had been done to me and the other girls was wrong. But maybe, just maybe, it wasn't all as black and white as I'd thought. Luca had fought for me, and he'd paid steeply for it. Who was to say someone else hadn't done the same? Surely, somewhere on this island, at least one other person had fought for me. Had at least spoken up for me, for the others.

Children would have been born since I'd left. Did I really want to condemn them, to condemn everyone, to the Darkness because I was too pissed to do something about it?

I still wasn't convinced by the whole prophecy bullshit—I didn't think I ever would be—but I was a *Hunter*. And the entire damn territory might seemed to have forgotten what that meant, but I hadn't.

So no one else wanted to fight this thing? Fine. *I* would fight it. And if what Luca had said to the Elders was any indication, he would have my back.

"No," I answered aloud, "I don't have any intention of doing what they say."

Devryn grinned. "Good."

"The Darksickness. No one knows how it happens?"

Devryn shook his head. "There's no rhyme or reason to it. Some people get bit by Dark creatures and never come down with it, some people have no contact with the Dark at all and get sick. Some people get better, some don't. The healers can't make heads or tails of it."

"How long does it take to kill?"

"The longest anyone's lasted after they fall unconscious is a week."

"And my father?"

"Wouldn't wake up this morning."

I stared at my father, lying in bed, helpless in a way I had never seen him. "Can I ask you a question?"

"Can't guarantee I'll answer, but sure."

"Why haven't you killed him?" From the way Devryn had spoken about my Dad, from the situation he'd described, it didn't sound like there was any true love lost between them.

"Do you wish I would?"

"No." I was furious at my dad, but I didn't want him dead. Mostly, I wanted him to wake up and tell me he was sorry. That he'd been wrong to tell me to leave, to not do anything to stop the Elders from banishing me. I wanted him to tell me he regretted his decision. I didn't honestly think there was a chance in hell of him doing so, but I wanted him to. Barring that, I wanted at least the *chance* to yell at him. To tell him he'd been wrong.

"I...get along with your father," Devryn said, finally. "We understand each other. Maybe calling him a surrogate father's a stretch, but he's the closest thing I have to one. And even if his reasons for pulling me out of my situation were selfish, he did pull me out of them. He saw value in me when no one else did.

"If I lead Hunter someday it will be because he died of old age, not because I put a dagger in his back."

Oddly enough, the words made my lips tug up. It was a bitter smile, but it was still a smile.

"What?" Devryn asked. He said it a little sharply, as if he thought I was making fun of him with that smile.

"I was just thinking that if I had to have an adopted brother, you're not the worst I could have done."

"I'm so pleased I meet with your approval." It was sarcasm, obviously. I just couldn't tell if it was goodnatured or not.

"You know you don't have anything to worry about, right? Even if he did wake up and want to put me back in the lineup, I won't take it."

He stared at me, as if trying to figure out if I was lying or not. "Why?"

"I don't want it," I said truthfully. I never had. I loved what I was. I loved the legacy of power that ran in my veins, the skill that had been trained into me. But I had never wanted to lead Hunter. "And frankly, I hate everyone in this damn territory too much to lead them."

The other territories not personally having my back I'd understood. I wasn't *theirs*. But I had been Hunter's. And no one here had stood up for me. I couldn't *live* among that, much less lead it. "Hunter is yours, Devryn. Enjoy it." I turned away.

"What are you going to do?"

"First, I'm going to piss off some wolves." Turned out I had an itch to go to the pack's weekend bonfire after all. "Then I'm going to go looking for a fight in the Darkness."

I was ten feet away when he said, "If you need help in that fight, you've got it."

I turned back, raised an eyebrow. "I thought the Elders had a strict no-fighting-the-thing-trying-to-annihilate-our-island policy."

Devryn shrugged. "Offer stands."

I nodded. "Thanks."

"If you're going to piss off wolves," Devryn said casually, "do you want better weapons?"

I glanced at my knife. It wasn't a bad knife, considering what the mortal realm had to offer. It was, however, a single knife. My one, solitary weapon.

"As a matter of fact, I would."

❧ 21 ❧

LUCA

I SHOULD HAVE GUESSED ASH WOULD GO TO SEE HER FATHER. I should have offered to take her there myself but between Kiera, near-hypothermia, my father, and the Elders, somehow the thought had slipped my mind. If I'd walked into Hunter territory with her at my side, getting in wouldn't have been a problem.

Because I didn't have her, and because Gareth was with me, I got held up at the border on bureaucratic bullshit, and it took half an hour for them to let me through. You wouldn't think blacksmiths would be the type, but the two that worked at Hunter's borders loved playing gatekeeper. By the time I reach Barren Hunter's house I was already primed to explode, and catching Ash's scent tangled with another's, with a *man's*, had the wolf snarling in my chest.

I cleared the six steps to the front door in a single leap, my canines lengthening, claws bursting out the ends of my fingertips. I knocked on the door once, hard enough to put a hairline crack in the wood. When Devryn Ryder opened the door and I smelled Ash's scent on him, I suddenly didn't care that attacking him would start a territory feud.

"Where is she?" I demanded.

"Lost her already?" Devryn *tsked*. "You know what they say. If a woman runs away from you, straight into the arms of another man—"

I lost it. I lunged for him, my hand wrapping around his throat, and slammed him into the wall. Gareth grabbed me and hurled me off Devryn. *What the fuck?* The wolf in me didn't care *why* Gareth had intervened. It just wanted my teeth ripping out Devryn's throat, wanted to erase the scent that had twined with Ash's. The only scent that belonged on her was mine. *She* was mine, and—

Devryn's laughter cut through the red haze of fury, my surprise blunting the edges of my anger, just enough that I didn't immediately attack him again.

"*She* may have no intention of mating but you're already there, aren't you?"

An unexpected prick of pain sliced through me. Ash had told him she didn't want me? Why had they even talked about me? Why was she telling Devryn Ryder anything? The guy had taken her title, her father, her goddamn home. "Where. The fuck. Is she?" I asked. "And why is her scent all over you?"

I hadn't meant to ask the last part. I didn't really want to know. Because it suddenly occurred to me that Ash didn't really have a home in Elysium anymore. She didn't have any resources. And since she didn't want me, forming an alliance with Devryn made strategic sense.

"Before you answer that," Gareth said, "I'd advise you not to fuck with him anymore. It isn't in anyone's best interests right now."

Devryn snorted. "Who would have thought the pack trickster would be such a stick in the mud?"

If Devryn didn't start talking actual information in the

next five seconds, I was going to rip his throat out and nothing Gareth did was going to stop me.

"I didn't know who she was when she showed up. You have any idea how many would-be Hunter leaders I've fought off since the old man got sick? Thought she was just another challenger. We had a bit of a tussle before we sorted things out."

I gave him a skeptical once-over. "You fought Ashlynn and you're still alive?"

Devryn's jaw tightened. "She only won because she cheated. Knives aren't allowed in a challenge."

I laughed. "A fight's a fight. You win it or lose it."

Devryn flashed his teeth in mimicry of a smile. "You know, I think the old man had it right when he cut her out of the Hunter legacy. She thinks just like one of you."

I ignored the dig. Of course Ashlynn thought like a wolf. I'd taught her to. "What happened?" Was she inside? It didn't smell like she was inside.

"She wanted to talk to the old man but he's not waking up anymore. We confirmed she doesn't want her old title back and then I told her a sad, sad story about a teenage werewolf chained to the Elder Tree."

"You did *what*?"

"Just doing you a favor, man. Women love it when we get all tortured for them. Literally, in your case. And given her attitude when she showed up, it really seemed like you needed the help. By the way," he said, a little too casually, "have you seen her tattoo yet?"

Why would I care about her tattoos? "They're on her arms, why *wouldn't* I have seen them?"

Devryn grinned. "That's a no, then. Take her shirt off sometime. You might find it interesting."

The growl that tore out of me was in no way human. "Why the fuck would you know—"

"Did I mention she went that way?" He pointed at White Woods pack territory. "Said she had some wolves to piss off."

"Fuck." Devryn had no idea what he'd done. "How long ago?"

"Twenty minutes?"

Fuck, fuck, *fuck*. I jumped off the porch. Fur and fangs tore out of me in midair. I landed on four paws and took off for the woods.

22

ASHLYNN

SOMETHING WEIRD WAS GOING ON. I JUST COULDN'T QUITE pinpoint what it was. I stood in the Pack's town center, for lack of a better thing to call it, and contemplated the weird. Everything *seemed* normal. The usual bonfire, a supreme monument to werewolf idiocy, was roaring away, halfway between the forest and the Elder Tree.

Really, who built a fucking bonfire in a fucking forest? How had they never burned the whole territory down?

Then there was the Elder Tree itself. It towered so high I couldn't see the tops of the branches, its trunk wide enough it would take six people holding hands just to encircle it. Deep gouges and grooves ran the circumference, wounds that hadn't been there when I left.

How hard had Luca struggled that he'd left those marks? He'd been fifteen. And the entire pack had just let it happen. Just like they'd let me get banished. At least with me, they'd had the excuse of out of sight, out of mind. They didn't have that excuse with Luca. They'd walked through this clearing every day for *weeks* and seen the silver burning into his skin.

Had anyone even tried to stop it? My hands curled into fists at my sides.

"Hey."

I didn't jump, but it was a near thing. I'd been here for fifteen minutes and no one had spoken to me yet. Werewolves didn't really do subtlety, so I'd been on the receiving end of a lot of speculative looks no one bothered to hide, but no one had come up to me before now.

The woman who'd approached me had dark black skin and amber eyes fringed with thick lashes. Tight black curls framed a pretty, heart-shaped face.

"Remember me?" she asked.

I almost snapped that, no, of course I didn't, because it had been twelve years and everyone I used to know had gone from child to adult. But she just had this presence about her that said she was one of the nicest, most genuine people in the world, and I couldn't do it. I only remembered one person who fit that bill.

"Melody?" I hazarded a guess.

She smiled, a soft, brilliant glow that lit up her entire face. Behind her, I heard a collective groan go through a group of eight or so wolves. "You just won me a week off patrol duty."

"You bet on whether or not I'd remember who you were?"

"Why not?"

Werewolves. They really would bet on anything. I couldn't find it in myself to be mad at her. So what if a tiny, tiny part of me had hoped she'd approached me as a friendly gesture?

"Congratulations," I said drily. "So glad I could make your evening better."

"Honey, you made the whole week better. Come hang out with us." She slipped her arm in mine before I could argue and walked me back to the group that had been betting on my memory skills. Too late, I realized that group included Kiera. Pretty, perfect, polished Kiera.

She flashed me a smile that was all wolf, but the purr of her voice was all cat. It was an odd dichotomy in a werewolf. "You didn't bring Luca with you?" she asked innocently. "Don't tell me there's already trouble in paradise."

The guy who had his arm around her shoulders clearly didn't have enough brain cells to follow the very obvious dig she was making. He just looked confused and said, "You know Luca never comes to these things anymore. Not since—" He broke off, seeming to finally realize what he was saying as his gaze shifted from me to the Elder Tree and then back.

"Since what?" I asked sweetly.

He swallowed, audibly. "Nothing. Never mind."

"Since you all let him spend a month chained to a fucking tree?" I was pleased my voice came out dripping with saccharine sweetness when it wanted to boil over with rage.

It was Kiera who fixed me with a gaze that had more backbone in it than I ever would have given her credit for. "Don't act like you have any idea what it's like to live in this pack," she snarled.

"What's it like to live in this pack, sis?" A tall, broad-shouldered man with Kiera's light brown hair came up behind her. I thought I saw her tense, but I must have imagined it, because she was all smiles and laughter a second later.

"Like a dream." She smiled, her canines lengthening just a fraction. "One spoiled little Hunter children don't know anything about because they don't belong."

Her brother—she had two, Clay and Evan, though I didn't know which one this was—looked me over. I didn't particularly like the look.

"Well, if it isn't little Ashlynn Hunter, all grown up." There was a mountain's worth of innuendo in the *all grown up* part. "Where's Prince Lucy?"

Clay, then. He was the only one of Kiera's brothers stupid enough to call Luca "Lucy." He was the oldest of the Silvermoon brood, next in the beta line of succession. Werewolf inheritance was both a blood thing, and not. I'd had a pack history obsession in my youth, and the histories showed the pack could go generations quietly passing leadership from parent to child, or they could hit a period where constant infighting meant the title changed hands multiple times in less than a decade.

Part of it was that strength ran in blood, and it was rare for anyone to be born outside of the line of leadership who could physically challenge an alpha or beta. And part of it, I suspected, was fear. No one wanted to be the family whose brother/cousin/son challenged pack leadership, died, and left a stain on them. It had happened a couple times when I was here.

Neither of the challenger's surviving family lasted more than six months, every single one of them killed off in inter-pack squabbles.

Everyone was staring at me, and I remembered Clay had asked me a question. I'd sort of thought it was one that didn't deserve an answer, but then I'd forgotten that in the werewolf world, when someone from the beta's family asked a question, you answered it.

I shrugged, like I didn't care where Luca was, even though I was really starting to wish he was right next to me. "He and the Elders were feeling chatty. I wasn't."

"His loss, our gain." Clay smiled. It might have been charming—he was handsome enough—if it weren't for the fact it went nowhere near his eyes. They were green like Kiera's and, if possible, even less inviting. His voice, however, was all suggestive. "Let's get a drink."

I debated telling him to fuck off just for the fun of it. But while picking a werewolf fight was definitely what I was in the mood for, my rational brain told me I'd be better off trying to get information out of him. Clay had always been a bully, always needing to climb over people and take things away from them to make himself feel important, and it didn't appear he'd changed any.

He didn't see me as a person. He saw me as a thing to take away from Luca, a prophecy-named claim to fame. That was just fine. I could play dumb and begging to be stolen. As long as I kept my eager hands away from my newly-returned weapons, everything would be fine.

Around me, it felt like the pack held its collective breath. I wished I knew if it was because Clay was stepping into Luca's unofficial territory—and I *really* didn't like that I was back less than twelve hours and every wolf under the Elysian sun had decided I was Luca's territory—or if it was something else to do with this stupid prophecy.

I really needed to find out what the damn thing actually said. It might be made-up bullshit, but everyone here believed it, and it would obviously affect their actions.

"You're buying," I told Clay, in a cavalier voice that suggested I was too dumb to understand the tangled weave of pack politics I was stepping my foot into with that acceptance.

He nodded toward the pack bar, an establishment unoriginally named The Thirsty Wolf, and headed for it like my following him was his due in life. I suppressed an eye roll and waited until he was ten paces away to follow. When I did, Kiera stood, walking into my path as if I wasn't even there. She bumped my shoulder, hard, and I felt her hand slip into my pocket. "Watch where you're going," she snapped.

"Oh, fuck off," I shot at her retreating back. My hands itched to know what she'd put in my pocket—said pockets were too obviously empty for her to have been looking for something—but I waited until my back was to the group to shove my hands into my pockets. My fingertips brushed a piece of paper.

A note? *Kiera Silvermoon* had passed me an incognito note? What the hell?

I was almost to the bar before I got a chance to palm it and read. *Don't trust him.*

No shit, I thought. She'd went to the trouble of being sneaky to deliver *that* warning? Then again, she thought I was a spoiled princess and probably didn't think I had two brain cells to rub together. I guess I couldn't really blame her since I thought the same of her. Even if I was beginning to suspect otherwise.

She could be fucking with me—she *had* tried to kill me a handful of hours ago, and she wanted Luca—but somehow I didn't think she was. For one, I had a hard time seeing what she would gain from the warning. Then there was her snarled comment earlier, about me having no idea what it was like to grow up in the pack, before her brother had shown up and she'd glossed over all pretty and carefree.

I'd thought she'd flinched, when Clay had walked up. A suspicion formed and took root in the back of my mind, and I really didn't like it. Hating her would be so much easier.

At the bar—which was outdoor, like almost everything in the pack's "town center"—Clay looked like he was having a mild disagreement with the bartender, but by the time I arrived, Clay was carrying two drinks to one of the outdoor tables. I took a seat on one of the tree-trunk stools, and Clay joined me and slid a mug of beer across the table to me.

He lifted his own mug in the classic toast-giving position and said, "To your return."

I didn't need Kiera's note for all my female warning bells to scream, *Don't drink the beer.* I smiled, clinked my mug to his, and pretended to take a long swallow.

"So," Clay said, "what's life like in the mortal world?"

"Boring. Loud. Smells bad."

He raised an eyebrow. "That's it?"

"They do have better beer." I casually pushed mine away from me and watched the sharp bite of irritation roll across his irises. "And no one's getting chained up in the town square for trying to help a friend." At least, not in my corner of the mortal realm.

"Is that what Luca told you?"

I shrugged and didn't correct him on the source of my information. I was more interested in seeing where he'd take this.

"The truth is, he'd been chafing against Aiden's command for years. He needed to be put in his place, and Aiden finally did it."

I couldn't believe Clay was saying this out loud. In public. Where nearly the entirety of the pack could hear him. Even if Luca never came here anymore, he was still the heir to White Woods. Clay was talking about the wolf who was going to be his alpha some day. Unless...

"Luca could have taken that as the teaching moment it was meant as—"

Right. As if Aiden were a loving, fatherly sort who just wanted the best for his son.

"—but instead he reacted like a petulant child. Instead of working harder, he's been sulking in a cabin on the outskirts of our territory for the last twelve years. He barely knows the pack. He can't lead us if he doesn't know us."

Clay might have a point there, except I didn't for a second think he was actually concerned about the pack's wellbeing.

"And what does any of this have to do with me?" I asked, trying for genuine confusion. I don't think I would have fooled anyone less hopped up on his own self-importance. I'd never been very good at faking things I didn't feel.

"You were replaced as Hunter's heir. You're thinking being tied to Luca will elevate you back to the rank you lost."

Wow, Clay really didn't know me at all.

"It won't," he continued. "Luca's on his way out. He has been for years. If you want to be at the top of the hierarchy again, it's my side you want to be at."

"Is it?" I asked, unable to temper the coolness in my voice. He didn't notice. He nodded and leaned in, obviously thinking he was getting somewhere.

"I've been more of a son to Aiden than Luca ever has. The change in succession is all but official."

All but being the caveat. "And what would you get out of my...shifting alliance?"

"Aside from the obvious?"

His gaze swept over me, lingering on my breasts. Ugh, was I supposed to be flattered? Also, was I supposed to be an idiot? The pack boasted dozens of women prettier than me, all of whom didn't come with the baggage of being Hunter-born.

"Yes," I answered, "aside from that."

"Luca doesn't deserve you. He's a boy cringing at the edge of the woods because his daddy hurt his feelings. You're strong, and beautiful. You were raised to lead. You're the perfect mate for the next alpha. But that alpha won't be Luca. It *will* be me."

Right. I'm sure it has nothing to do with this stupid prophecy.

"Are you going to challenge him?" I asked. Luca would rip Clay apart. I'd seen them fight as kids. Clay was hot-tempered, volatile, and he didn't think things through. Luca was hot-tempered and volatile, but he had a brain. It gave him a distinct advantage.

"I won't have to," Clay answered. "Once you and I are together, Aiden will see there's no point in holding on to Luca anymore."

Translation, Aiden had promised Clay that if he could get me, Aiden would disinherit Luca in favor of him. But *why?* I'd thought I understood Aiden. He liked power, liked being associated with it. For that reason, I could see him wanting to be tied to the prophecy. But he *had* to know Luca had a hell of a lot better chance of getting me to stick around than this idiot did.

"So, what do you say?" Clay asked.

"You've given me a lot to think about." No lie there. "So I'll go home and think about it." I didn't have a home right now, but Luca's cabin would do. Because that wolf and I needed to have a serious discussion, wherein he finally gave me some damn answers instead of just growling at me, and I didn't let myself get too distracted or pissed off to extract them from him.

"I'll walk you," Clay offered when I stood.

"That isn't necessary." I walked for the edge of the clearing. Clay came with me.

"Maybe not. But the woods aren't the safest place right now. I'd hate it if something happened to you."

Clay Silvermoon's attempt at wooing, ladies and gentlemen. Insist on doing something the lady doesn't want, and top it off with a thinly veiled threat.

You know what? Fine. "That's sweet of you." Let's see what he did when he walked me right to Luca's door. I moved into the woods, orienting myself in the direction of Luca's cabin. It had been a long time since I'd explored the White Woods, so I might come out a little too far in one direction or the other, but I thought I could peg it within a half-mile.

Clay didn't talk, which both suited me just fine and filled me with unease. There was an odd energy coming off him that felt clipped. Not as if he was afraid, but as if he was psyching himself up to do something.

I considered that he might try to kidnap me. It wasn't outside the realm of possibility, and it would send Luca absolutely ballistic. If he wanted to make Luca seem even more unhinged, taking me would be the perfect way to do it.

Only one way to find out. I stopped walking, and that was when I realized how dead quiet the woods were. We'd come far enough that we would be out of hearing range of the wolves in the clearing. Just me, and Clay, and whatever lurked in the approaching night.

I rested my hand on my hip, right next to the hilt of my dagger. "Why are you really out here with me, Clay?"

"Isn't it obvious?" He grabbed me roughly and forced his mouth on mine. I didn't open for him and the crush of his assault split my lower lip. His tongue shoved at my teeth, trying to gain entrance. I kept my mouth clenched shut and pulled back.

I didn't get far, just enough to tear my lips from his. His arms had locked in a bear hug around my waist, trapping my arms inside the hold. He was almost as big as Luca, and struggling only served to make him excited. The evidence of which I had no choice but to feel, given he'd locked me to him.

"Let me go, Clay. I'm not interested."

He didn't let me go. I stretched my fingers for my knife hilt. His hold on me was so brutal it was cutting off the circulation to my arms. If I didn't reach the blade now, soon I wouldn't be able to.

"What is it with women?" Clay snarled. "You always say you're not interested and you always end up underneath me anyway." He pressed against me and I gagged, hot bile spilling up my throat.

The panic that spilled through me almost overcame all reason. It was the instinctual need of the hunted to flee, the violation of being touched when I didn't want it, the knowledge that if I couldn't break free of this, more than touching would occur.

I had never feared rape in the mortal realm. Because no matter how strong a mortal man, *I* would always be stronger. I had never had to know the unease that made women carry car keys likes blades between their fingers, made them second-guess what they wore when they should be able to wear whatever they damn well pleased. Never had to worry that even if I did everything right, took all the precautions, fought as hard as I could, that *this* could still happen to me.

But I'd been safe in my superiority for too long. Werewolves were *strong*. Stronger than a Hunter missing her Heartstone. A fresh wave of panic slammed into me and I struggled blindly, which only served to further arouse Clay.

I stopped fighting him. *Think, damn it. You're a Hunter.*

Clay chuckled, breath hot against my ear. "That's it. You want it, don't you?"

I held my breath so I wouldn't tell him what I really thought. If he wanted to take my clothes off, he'd have to release me, at least partially. And if he thought I wanted it...

I let out my held breath, forced myself to relax, and rubbed my nose in the hollow at the base of his throat. I couldn't bring myself to kiss him. Even this little voluntary brush of skin almost made me vomit. Especially when he humped against me.

"I knew you wouldn't be hard to take away from him." He bit the side of my neck and then his hold loosened, one of his hands fumbling for the front of my jeans. My near-numb fingers brushed the hilt of my dagger. I tore the blade free and plunged it into his back.

It was surprise, I think, more than pain that had him shoving me away from him so hard my feet left the ground. My back slammed into the trunk of a tree and I dropped to the ground, trying desperately to work feeling back into my numb wrists and hands.

"I was trying to make it easy for you," Clay snarled, ripping my dagger out of his back. The blade wasn't silver, so what little damage it had done would already be healing over. "Remember that when you're screaming."

Magic tore from him, enveloping me in a sticky swathe that burned against my skin like acid, contracting around me like a shrinking cocoon. It stabbed at the defenses I'd instinctively thrown up, whispering one word over and over: *mine, mine, mine.*

Mating bond. The son of a bitch was trying to force a *mating bond* on me. I poured everything I had into my hasty barrier, my own power slicking over me like a protective coating. The bond tore at me, burned especially strong at those places where Clay had touched me, as if his unwanted kisses and gropes gave him some right, some claim to me.

In his mind, they likely did.

My lips felt like someone had dumped gasoline on them and lit a match.

My hands pricked and tingled with the needle-stabs of returning life. Clay advanced even as his power crushed me like a vise. He was *strong*, the pull of the mating bond fierce, and I could feel every disgusting desire he had through it.

He *wanted* me, wanted me bound and subservient. He wanted to make me pay for the knife I'd put in his back, to break me. Wanted to take me and shove it in Luca's face. All that hate and fury and desire to dominate crushed down on me like a collapsing building. The weight of it pushed the air from my lungs and I knew if it succeeded, I'd never be able to breathe again.

Because if it succeeded, I'd never be *me* again.

I forced myself to take that breath. It hurt, like razorblades cutting down my throat as I inhaled. Moving hurt more. My fingers stretched toward my other dagger, and it felt like sticking my hand into the pack's bonfire. But when my fingers closed over the hilt, I didn't care how it seared me, how my palm burned and begged me to release the weapon as if it were a live coal.

I pulled the blade free as Clay's fingers closed around my

throat. He hauled me to my feet and slammed my bruised back against the tree. His forearm ran the length of my chest, his weight bearing against me as he leaned in.

His free hand grabbed for the wrist that held my dagger but I was already moving, driving the blade into his stomach. When I'd stabbed him the first time, we'd both been off guard. Numb fingers had made me drop my weapon, and surprise had made him hurl me away.

This time he just grunted as the blade slid in, squeezing my throat with werewolf strength until white spots danced in my vision. His other hand wrapped around my wrist. Claws erupted from his fingertips, piercing my neck, thick spikes driving into one side of my wrist and out the other.

The bloodlust whipped his power into a frenzy, wave upon wave of it crashing over me, demanding that I give up, give in, submit. How much did he *have*? How much did *I* have? If I had my Heartstone, this wouldn't even be a contest. But without it, I was limited in what power I could access.

I couldn't feel my right hand, wasn't sure how I kept hold of the dagger, kept it plunged in Clay's stomach. Wasn't sure what kept him from ripping it out, except that all his power, all his focus, seemed to be given over to a desperate bid to make the mating bond take.

If it didn't...what happened then?

I rallied my strength—all my power, all my anger, all my refusal to be owned—and hurled it at him. The cocoon of power around me stuttered. Pulsed. Shattered.

Clay howled in pain. His hands ripped free of me to clutch at his head and I slumped to the ground, sucking in huge lungfuls of air and willing the brightness in my vision to clear. I blinked through it and looked at my hands. The dagger was still in my right, though I couldn't feel it, blood pouring from the puncture wounds in my wrist.

Hunters didn't heal as fast as wolves, but we healed faster

than mortals, and as I watched the blood began to clot, the flow to stem.

Move. I had to move. Before Clay recovered from whatever pain throwing off the mating bond had caused. I reached over with my good hand and grasped the dagger. Staggered to my feet.

I lunged and drove the blade between his ribs. I was a Hunter, and my aim was true, tip piercing through to strike the heart. My legs gave out. I dropped back to the ground, content to watch Clay die slowly.

But the white blur that shot from the forest, knocking Clay to the ground, had no such contentment. Luca closed his massive jaws over Clay's throat and snapped them shut. The sharp crack of a neck snapping filled the unnaturally quiet forest air.

But Luca didn't stop there. Lost in a frenzy, he bit and tore, bit and tore, until Clay's head came free of his body in a mess of blood and bone and cartilage.

I think he would have kept going, would have torn Clay's body to shreds too small to ever identify, if I hadn't tried to rise and fallen back to my knees when my vision receded at the edges again.

Luca was at my side in an instant, his white muzzle stained with blood, a low whine in his throat.

"It's fine," I managed, sheathing the dagger and burying my fingers in the thick fur around his neck. I did it for him, obviously, not because *I* needed the support. Which I totally didn't. I would remember how to breathe again any second, and I would stop freaking out about whether I'd permanently lost the use of my right hand. I healed faster than mortals, but right now I would kill to heal like a werewolf.

"Everything's fine," I repeated. A growl rumbled low in Luca's throat, a clear disagreement if ever I heard one. His wet nose pushed against my injured arm. He licked at the wounds and the soft warmth of power spread into me, healing and soothing, almost as if—almost as if he were lending me a werewolf's swift ability to heal.

That wasn't possible. Was it? He couldn't just *give me* his healing power. But even as I thought it the pain receded. The wounds closed, scabbed over. Then the scabs flaked off, revealing fresh, new skin beneath them. I stared and flexed my fingers in disbelief.

"How did you *do* that?" I'd never heard of anything like it.

Luca didn't answer. His gaze went to the sky between the trees and focused on the sun. The setting sun.

Shit. The Darkness. I hadn't even thought about it, wasn't used to having to take into account that being out after dark could actually be dangerous. Luca didn't bother with charades this time, like he had after we climbed out of the ocean. He just circled behind me, dropped to his belly, and crawled between my legs. Then he lunged to his feet, lifting me off the ground, and took off. The only option I had was to clamp my legs around him and hold on.

He flew through the woods, his massive paws churning up clods of earth in his wake. The wind created by his speed chapped at my face, made my eyes sting with tears. He dodged between trees, leaped over fallen brush and deep ravines, tearing a path to his cabin at the wood's edge.

The edge of the forest was in sight, Luca's cabin a mere fifteen feet beyond it, when shadows dropped from the trees.

But I was ready for the Slithers this time. I clung tighter to Luca with my legs and drew my dagger, my right arm up so if one tried to boa constrict me again I'd have my arm between it and my neck. I was officially over being choked.

I hacked at falling bodies with the dagger, grabbed and flung with my free hand, fending off one after another.

Luca tore out of the woods and the rain of Slithers stopped. Two were still attached to us, jaws clamped into wolf fur, one on Luca's right shoulder, the other on his left foreleg. I grabbed the wriggling body attached to his shoulder and severed the head, pried the clamped jaws free and flung the mouth away.

Luca cleared the steps to his cabin in a single bound. I jumped from his back and made quick work of the second Slither. I'd only just torn its fangs free when Luca shifted, wrenched the front door open, and shoved me inside.

I'd barely caught my footing when the door closed behind me and Luca hauled me up against it. I had a flashback to Clay shoving me against the tree and shuddered.

Luca stilled and took a step back. "Are you hurt?" he demanded.

I tried to find words and couldn't. My body flashed hot then cold, hot then cold, like I was in the grip of a fever.

"Are. You. Hurt?" Luca repeated.

"N-no." My teeth were chattering.

"You're in shock." He moved forward to take me in his arms, then stopped, hesitating.

The smell of it must have been all over the woods, all over *me*—what Clay had wanted, what he'd tried to do to me. And now Luca was afraid to touch me. Now I was shivering and remembering hands I hadn't wanted touching me.

No. Clay didn't get to do that to me. He didn't get to take that from me. He'd tried, and now he was dead, and I needed to purge him.

Luca practically vibrated with the need to touch me, to assure himself that I was okay. I launched myself at him, crushing my mouth to his. It was less of a kiss, more of a statement, a hot, desperate claiming.

"Ash," he growled when we came up for air. "We need to think about—"

I nipped at his lower lip, then soothed the small hurt with the glide of my tongue.

"Ashlynn."

I had never been more grateful for post-change werewolf nudity than in this moment. I ran my hands over the firm muscles of his chest, down the hard planes of his abs, and finally lower, where the massive length of him was hard and throbbing. I took him firmly and squeezed. I trailed kisses up his jaw, sucked at the lobe of his ear. "Fuck me, Luca."

He groaned and thrust into my hand. I didn't think the movement was voluntary and I needed that, needed him helplessly mad for me, needed to feel the power of making him that way.

"Baby." His voice was low and rough, a plea and a prayer. "I'm not going to be able to walk away, soon."

"I don't want you to walk away." I pumped my hand once up and down his erection. "I want you to erase him."

He stilled completely, and I needed him to move. Against me, with me, in me. I kept my hand fisted around him, rocked onto my toes and nipped my way from his strong jaw down to his collarbone, where I bit and sucked until a bruise appeared for the shortest time before werewolf healing took it away.

"Ash," he groaned.

"Luca," I purred back. He wasn't losing control, and I wanted him to. I wanted him to take me right against the damn door and fuck me so hard I saw stars. I thumbed the slit at the head of his cock. It was slick with pre-come and I rubbed it over him, felt him jerk in my hand.

"Mmm, that's what I like," I said. "You, hard and ready."

He moved then. He grabbed my wrists with one hand and held them above my head, his hips pinning mine against the door. A small tremor of fear licked through me and I fought it back, refused to give into it.

But instead of kissing me or ripping my clothes off, Luca buried his face in the curve of my neck and breathed me in, like he was still fighting for control. "You're not thinking clearly," he told my neck, dropping his hands down to cradle my hips.

Anger pulsed through me, hot and vicious. "I'm thinking just fine, Luca. If you don't want me, all you have to do is say so."

He cursed. "It's not that, and you damn well know it."

"Is it Kiera?" I almost choked on her name. When Devryn had told me that story about Luca I'd just assumed—but wanting to keep a promise to me wasn't the same as wanting *me*. "Are you wishing I was her?"

"*No*." He dragged his head up from my neck and held my gaze. "I told you, I haven't been with her in months. *You* are the only person I want to be with."

"Then what's the problem?"

"If sex is what you need right now, I'll give it to you." He swallowed. "But I don't just want to give you a night. I don't know if I *can* just give you a night. I want you to want *me*. Not a temporary escape."

His eyes, dark and filled with longing, held nothing back. They contained everything I'd wanted, dreamed, of seeing there.

"But if that's not something you can give me, I just need to know. Before we do this."

I swallowed. I wasn't good at laying my cards on the table. Honesty, emotional intimacy, wasn't something I'd ever done with a man before. I might not have realized it, or I might have just been lying to myself, but I'd been saving that for him. For Luca.

But now that he was here, asking for it, I didn't know how to give it to him. Not with words. But then, maybe I didn't have to use words.

I reached for his hand and drew it to my heart, under the collar of my V-neck, and pressed his palm flat to my skin. My pulse quickened, all my insecurities rising to the surface at the idea of showing him what lay beneath.

But I couldn't hide it forever. And I couldn't doubt him forever. I had doubted that he'd tried to come for me, and he had the scars to prove it.

He wouldn't laugh at me over this. Because he was Luca and I was Ash, and we belonged together. We always had.

"I want *you,* Luca." I took a deep breath and curled his fingers around my shirt collar. "See for yourself."

He hesitated, then pulled my shirt aside, baring his name in all its scrollwork-lettered glory on my heart.

His eyes went so hot they were practically molten. He snapped and lunged for me.

23

LUCA

Seeing my name on Ash's heart like a brand, like a mark of absolute possession, sent a pulse of pure need straight to my dick. It told me everything I needed to know, everything I'd hoped for.

Me. She wanted me. Not just a body to make her forget what Clay had almost done to her. I wanted to bring him back to life so I could kill him again, and as I thought it, I realized *I* needed to erase him, too.

I needed to hold Ash, to taste her and feel her and prove to myself that she was here, and alive, and whole. I grabbed her waist and pulled her to me, needing to rub my aching hard-on between her legs, to feel the taste of her against my mouth.

She was ten steps ahead of me. She wrapped her legs around my waist and rocked against me, the friction from her jeans and the slight pain from the rough fabric sending all the blood in my body dangerously south. Her mouth was hot and hungry. She kissed and licked and bit me until I was in a near frenzy.

"Need you naked," I said between kisses. "And underneath me."

"Agreed."

I cupped her ass and squeezed, walked her into the bedroom and dumped her on the mattress. She tore off her shirt, reached back and unclasped her bra, shrugging it off to bare her breasts. Her nipples were already hard and pebbled. I sank to my knees and closed my mouth over one, swirling my tongue around the stiff peak before sucking, hard.

She let out a moan that had me throbbing and arched her hips against my waist.

"What happened to naked?" she panted.

I moved to her other breast, but my hands roamed lower, over the gloriously soft skin of her stomach, to unfasten her pants. I released her nipple to yank her pants down, pulling them off with her shoes until the only thing she wore was the lacy green thong she'd taunted me in that morning.

My hands slid to the insides of her knees and pushed her legs wide. The small scrap of cloth between her legs was dark where her moisture had soaked it through.

"I love how wet you get for me." I raked my hands up her thighs, felt her tremble when my thumbs teased at her panties.

"Take them off, Luca. I want you inside me."

"And I will be," I promised. "But I need to know how you taste, first." I'd been fantasizing about this since the moment I'd seen her, all grown up and so fucking hot I'd wanted to bend her over that damn bar and take her in a room full of strangers.

I took the ridiculously flimsy fabric in my hands and ripped it, baring her beautiful, glistening pussy. Then I buried my face in her and thrust my tongue straight into her hot, tight channel. She gasped and bucked against me. She fisted her fingers in my hair and writhed, her pussy contracting.

I licked up her center, took the bud of pleasure at the apex of her thighs into my mouth and sucked.

"Luca," she screamed.

I growled against her and circled her clit with my tongue. I wanted to make her scream my name again. And again, and again.

But she tightened her grip on my hair and dragged my face up. "Want," she said breathlessly, "to come on your cock."

"Fuck yes."

I'd barely climbed onto the bed before she shoved me onto my back and straddled me. She took my shaft in her hand and slid the head through the wetness coating her folds before positioning me at her entrance. She sank a mere inch onto me and moaned, the throaty noise making me jerk. Her pussy gave an answering spasm that almost had me losing it and thrusting up into her.

As if she could sense it she leaned forward, splaying her hands across my chest, tilting her hips at an angle that denied me further access. "How do you want it, baby?" she asked. "Do you want it soft and sweet?" She drew her finger in a light line down my chest, a smirk on her lips as if she already knew the answer to the question.

"No," I bit out.

She leaned back, trailed her hands down my stomach, her fingers playing at the base of my cock. "Do you want it slow and easy?"

I brought my hands up to grip her hips, unable to *not* touch her. "No."

"Then do you want it like this?" She thrust down, impaling herself on me in one hard, deep movement that seated me inside her.

"Ash." Her name was a prayer, a need, a benediction. It was twelve years of pent-up longing and not really understanding what I was longing for. It was knowing that she was the other half of myself and I'd lost her once, and there hadn't been a damn thing I'd been able to do about it.

My hands tightened, my fingers digging into her flesh as I struggled not to thrust into her, not to lose myself as deep in her as possible, to give her time for her body to adjust to me. But she *liked* the bite of my grip. She moaned and threw her head back, her eyes half-closing as her inner walls clenched around me.

"Fuck, baby." The smallest movement from her brought me perilously close to losing it, to flipping our positions and fucking her so thoroughly she didn't remember any other man existed and didn't want to.

Mine. She was *mine.* And as I thought it a tidal wave of power crashed through me, the mating bond demanding release. It could *make* her mine. Could wrap around her and claim her, a brand in truth instead of symbolism.

If she bore *my* bond, no wolf would dare come near her again. No more Clays trying to mate with her in the woods, no more threats from Aiden. She would be mine and I would always know where she was, when she was in danger. The Elders couldn't send her away again, not without me.

Do it. The power of the bond howled and screamed like a maelstrom inside me. This was right. *She* was right. She and I, together. It was inevitable, it always had been. The only thing I had to do was—

—force her.

I clamped down on the power that demanded release, chained it inside me with iron will, disgust slamming through me.

I wasn't any better than Clay, my instincts driving me to do the same fucking thing he'd tried. But I had a better chance of succeeding than he had. Because my cock was sheathed in Ash's pussy, every line of her open and welcoming.

If that power ripped out of me it would claim, and she would let it before she even realized what was even happening.

I bit the inside of my cheek until blood, bright and coppery, spilled over my tongue. I was a man, not a monster. I would *never* force her. Not to keep her, not to protect her, not for anything.

❧ 24 ❧

ASH

LUCA'S SKIN FLUSHED HOT BENEATH ME A SECOND BEFORE he went completely still, and all the fire and lust in his eyes vanished. I stilled, too, trying to figure out what had happened, why he'd gone from eager to empty.

"Hey. What happened?"

He didn't answer immediately, just breathed in and out, his massive chest rising and falling in shallow waves. "Nothing," he said.

"Mm-hmm." I folded over, resting my forearms on his chest and my chin on my hands, and trying not to moan in pleasure at the way it shifted his cock inside me. *Focus.* Because his body might be here but he wasn't, and if his cock was the only thing present I might as well be at home with a toy. "You're a bad liar, Luca. You were here and now you're not."

He didn't answer. My emotions, fragile and battered from being tossed every which way in the last twenty-four hours, took more of a beating than they should have from his silence.

It was stupid, but from the moment I'd tackled him in my

apartment complex's courtyard and understood who he was, I'd known that sex between us would be magical. Perfect.

But his cock was buried in me and I felt neither of those things. This wasn't perfection. This was distance and cold and silence, and how could I be feeling all of those things when our bodies were connected, when he was so deep inside me I didn't know where he ended and I began?

I waited for him to say something—anything—but he didn't. Tears pricked at the backs of my eyes. This was ridiculous. I shouldn't be naked and on him and about to fucking cry. Not after everything I'd been through tonight.

I sat up. I tried to get off him but his hands on my hips held me firmly in place.

"Ash." His voice was a mixture of plea and pain. "Don't go."

"Why the hell would I stay when you're already gone?" I snapped.

"I'm here."

"Then why does it feel like you're a million miles away?" My voice broke and the stupid, useless tears spilled down my cheeks. All my desire was officially gone, and I just wanted to run away.

"Fuck, baby." Luca cupped my face in his hands, the rough pads of his thumbs brushing away my tears. It was a futile gesture, because they just kept falling.

"Every time I think you can't hurt me again, you do."

"I'm sorry. I'm so fucking sorry." He lifted me up, off him, pulled me down so we lay face-to-face. He twined his legs in mine and locked his arm around my back like he was afraid I'd run if given half the chance. It was a reasonable fear.

"Sorry doesn't fix anything." Sorry didn't explain to me what had happened in the blink of an eye. It didn't tell me why, even though his eyes were expressing regret, he still felt cold and closed-off. All "sorry" meant was that he didn't like seeing me cry and that—that was just the natural discomfort anyone felt in the presence of someone else's pain.

"I know."

"You don't have to want me, Luca." I hated how raw I sounded, how broken. But I'd denied myself true intimacy the entirety of my life. I'd never gotten close to anyone, because even when I'd hated Luca, my heart had always been his. And he just kept breaking it.

"I want you, baby. I want you so bad I can't stand it. That's the problem." He swallowed. "If you understood what I wanted to do to you just now, you'd run away and you'd never come back. And maybe you should. Maybe you should feel everything I feel right now."

He took my hand in his and guided it to his chest, let it hover above his Heartstone. The jewel was still glamoured from sight, making his chest appear mortal-human. But no glamour could change a Heartstone's nature. They were conduits to those who bore them, and if I pressed my palm to Luca's, I would know every emotion that rode him.

And he was giving me permission.

"If you want to," he said hoarsely. Even this, he left up to me. I pressed my palm flat to his chest, and felt. I couldn't feel the Heartstone itself, even the touch of the stone had been glamoured away, but I felt *him*. Luca.

A surge of emotions crashed over me: Want and need. Longing and regret. Happiness and sorrow. Hope and guilt.

His want and need for me were like an ocean, wave upon wave that wouldn't stop, had *never* stopped. He'd longed for me since the day I'd left—for the friendship we'd had, for the life he'd expected we would grow into together.

The regret was harsher, steeper, the constant nagging belief that if he'd only been smarter, if he'd fought harder, he could have stopped the Elders from sending me away.

Happiness was a bright speck in the midst of a roiling sea

of darkness—happiness that I was alive. That I was here. That I was *home*. That I didn't hate him.

Sorrow, because it wasn't right, but I couldn't puzzle out what the *it* was.

Hope that maybe, even after all the years of distance, we could still be what we should have always been. That we could still be an *us*, that I might want the man he'd become in my absence.

Guilt, because in the moment I'd joined with him, the need to claim me had awakened so powerfully he'd almost let the mating bond tear out of him. Guilt, because even now, he still wanted it. Wanted to be mated. To me. Wanted to mark me in a way no other wolf could ever misunderstand, so they would always know that I was *his*, and crossing me meant crossing him.

So nothing like Clay could ever happen to me again.

He'd wanted it so badly he'd shut down, closed himself off to contain that need. But the bond still raged inside him, even now, demanding release.

"Oh, Luca," I whispered. He'd shut his eyes the moment my palm pressed to him. He hadn't wanted to see the horror he'd been certain he would find in my face. Because he thought he was just like Clay. "Open your eyes."

When he did, when his ice blue eyes were looking into mine, I kissed him. Surprise flitted through him but he kissed me back, and the need inside him crested, built, like a volcano threatening to erupt.

"Ash." His voice was ragged and harsh. "It's driving me senseless. I can't hold it."

"You're an idiot, Luca Ferrar," I said softly, gently.

"I'm aware. Perhaps you could explain in what particular way at the moment."

"When we were younger, when Mira and Celeste mated, I asked you what the mating bond was. Before you gave me a lecture on the numerous reasons never to do it, you explained that the bond that came from each wolf was a true expression of his or her self.

"You're an idiot, because I *know* you. I feel you, right now. You would never force me to do anything. And I can prove it to you. You don't have to fight the bond, Luca. Let it out. Nothing is going to happen."

He shook his head, even as the force of magic within him railed against his control, wanting exactly what I'd told him to do.

"You don't want to be mated to me," he said.

"Whether I do or don't is mine to decide. But I promise you that, for today, I won't be. Let it out, Luca. Let me show you who you are."

"No."

I kissed him again, rougher this time, needier. I licked and teased him, nipping at his bottom lip, at his jaw, down his neck, and all the while I kept my hand pressed to his Heartstone, felt the insistent pulse of magic grow stronger and stronger.

My free hand roamed down his stomach, to the shaft that had grown hard again when I kissed him. I took him in my hand and pumped him, once.

"Ash. I can't hold it."

"I don't want you to." I looked him in the eye and pumped him again, watched his eyes go hot and wild. "Tell me to stop and I will."

I waited.

"Don't stop," he whispered hoarsely. I felt his intentions through his Heartstone, his need to prove to himself that he could control it. And I needed to prove to him that he didn't have to.

I lowered myself and took him in my mouth, ran my tongue across the thick vein that throbbed on the underside of his shaft. He made a strangled noise and bucked against me. His hot tip hit the back of my throat and he wasn't even halfway inside me.

I loved the taste of him, the iron-hard length of him in my mouth. On another day, I'd spend the time to make him come just like this, to make him lose control and fuck my mouth until he spilled himself down my throat.

The thought made a little hum of pleasure escape me, and he throbbed in my mouth in response to the vibrations. I slid my mouth up him, tongued the slit at his head and licked up the salty drops of pre-come.

He growled, and one of the tethers of his control broke. He fisted his hands in my hair and jerked me up to his mouth, kissing me with a ferocity that would leave deliciously bruised lips in the morning. I rolled onto my back next to him and dragged him on top of me, needing the weight of him, knowing the wolf's need to dominate would drive him just a little wilder, a little hotter, in this position.

I tilted my hips up and ground my wetness against his length, the contrast of his hardness to my softness sending a spike of unadulterated pleasure through me. I slid my hand between us, coated my fingers in my own desire and ran them around his cock, until he was as slick as I was.

"All of that is for you, Luca. How wet you make me, how much I want you." His hands fisted into the sheets on either side of me. "I said it wasn't, but when I fucked myself in the shower this morning, that was for you, too. It was everything I could do not to scream your name."

He groaned. I positioned him at my entrance, and he shuddered. "Show me how much you want me," I ordered. "Make me feel it."

He drove into me in a hard, controlled thrust that made my toes curl. There was no pain this time. I'd had him inside me minutes before and my body knew the shape of him now, welcomed him. He buried himself to the hilt and I flexed my inner walls around him wanting, needing, more.

"Ash."

"I love it when you say my name." I rocked my hips up, felt him shift deep within me. I scraped my fingernails up his back and he shuddered again. "I love the way you fit with me, the way you touch me." I guided his hands to my breasts, writhed and moaned when he squeezed them. I looked into his eyes. "I'm yours, Luca Ferrar. I always have been."

He lost it. The wolf took over his eyes entirely, and he withdrew and rammed back in so hard his balls slapped against me.

"Yes," I breathed. "That's how I want it. Fuck me, Luca." He did, pistoning into me again and again, his big body pushing my legs wide, his massive length stretching every inch of me. I locked my legs around his hips as he rode me, needing his pleasure, his release.

But if I was unconcerned with my own in that moment, Luca wasn't. His hand came between us, his thumb stroking my clit as he drove tirelessly into me. My pleasure, already built and primed by the glide of his cock, by the feel of his body dominating mine, grew to an unbearable ache.

Luca's breathing grew harsh and ragged, his thrusts erratic. His thumb dragged across my clit again. "Come for me, baby," he demanded. His words, the raw need in them, and the roughness of his thumb working me sent me over the edge. My climax tore through my body, so hard I bowed off the bed, my pussy clamping around his cock with violent desire.

"Luca." I shouted his name, so loud it hurt my own ears. He roared and pumped into me one final time, his entire body jerking. And as he spilled himself into me, Luca Ferrar finally lost all control. The mating bond snapped out of him, surrounded me, a cocoon of light and magic and desire.

It slid against my skin, warm and sweet. But where Clay's bond had burned, had sought to force me to submit to him, to control me, Luca's only caressed. It was an extension of *him*, and he didn't want to own me. He wanted me to choose him.

It took everything I had not to accept what that bond offered. Not to let it in, to let it merge with me, to let it bind us together so intricately we could never be undone again. Because I wanted to. I wanted what it offered, the promise of never being alone again.

But there were two very good reasons not to. One, we still had a host of problems to solve, and getting myself mated in the middle of them, especially when I was pretty sure there were things Luca still wasn't telling me, sounded like a spectacularly bad idea. Two, if I accepted the bond now, Luca would never believe he hadn't forced it on me. Wouldn't understand that he *couldn't*.

He hadn't even realized he'd let it out, and I needed him to.

"Luca," I said, and kissed him. Softly, deeply. I felt the moment he realized what had happened. He tried to recoil but my legs, my arms, were still wrapped around him and I held him firm. "*Look*," I ordered. "Feel. I'm not trapped, Luca. And you aren't trying to cage me."

The mating bond flowed from him to me, dancing along my skin, wrapping around me and offering. *Only* offering. Like a companion that would wait beside me as long as I wanted, as long as it took, for me to be ready. And if I never was, it would simply keep waiting.

Luca's eyes widened. "I don't understand."

I smiled. "It's a reflection of you, Luca. And this is who you are. Good and perfect, and mine. You are mine, aren't you?"

"I'm yours," he said roughly.

"Good." I wiggled my hips against him, felt him start to harden again inside me.

He kissed me, hard and swift. "I've always been yours."

"Then show me," I ordered.

So he did.

25

ASHLYNN

I HADN'T MEANT TO FALL ASLEEP LAST NIGHT, BUT A FEW rounds of mind-blowing sex has a way of wrecking a girl's plans. I woke up spooned against Luca, his arm banded around my waist, holding me tight, his leg thrown over mine, and his massive morning wood pressed against my backside.

It was...strange, waking up with someone. Waking up with *him*. I placed my hand over his where it rested on my stomach and stroked my thumb over the ridged scarring around his wrist.

To make that much scar tissue on a werewolf, to leave not only a visible mark, but such a defined one...*Way I heard it, Luca almost tore through his wrists trying to get free.*

"You haven't asked about it," Luca said, his voice rough and thick from sleep.

"I didn't know you were awake."

"Wasn't." He nuzzled the side of my neck and squeezed me a little more tightly to him.

"I'm sorry," I said, softly.

He stilled. "For what?"

"For thinking the worst of you. For never giving you a chance to refute it."

"You only thought the truth. I promised I wouldn't let them send you away without me. I broke that promise."

"We were kids, Luca. It wasn't your problem to fix. Wasn't a problem you *could* have fixed."

He was quiet for a moment, his fingers teasing lazy circles on my stomach. "If I'd challenged my father instead of asking him for help, it would have been a different story."

My heart rabbit-kicked inside my chest. "Yes, it would. You'd be dead, and I'd be alone right now." The thought terrified me, and the part of me that was used to being alone, to not getting attached, wanted very much to jump to my feet and run away, so that I'd never again feel the panic beating through me right now, the fear of losing him.

"So little faith in me." Luca smiled against the curve of my neck and ground against me, his physical morning interest completely at odds with the unpleasant conversation we were having. It elicited an answering twinge between my legs that I fought to ignore. "I could have replaced Aiden by the time I was fourteen."

"I saw you two fight this morning," I reminded him.

"You saw me blowing off steam." His fingers trailed up my ribcage, stopped just at the underside of my breast as a thought seemed to occur to him. "Wait, did you jump in the middle of our fight because you were *worried* about me?"

"No," I lied. "I just didn't want a perfectly onerous morning interrupted with the excitement of bloodshed."

"You *were*." Luca chuckled and closed his hand over my breast. I tried not to move, not to make encouraging sounds, but it was difficult when his rough hand was palming me. "I like it when you worry about me." He punctuated this declaration by tweaking my nipple between his thumb and forefinger and I couldn't help it—I moaned and ground back against him.

"Do you want me this morning, Ashlynn?"

"Do you really need to ask?" I panted, having gone needy and achy in all the best ways. He had to be able to smell the arousal coming off me in waves.

"I do." He ground against me again, the rigid line of his cock pressing deliciously against the seam of my ass. "I like it when you say *yes*. It's my favorite word. So do you want me?"

"Yes." I guided his hand between my legs so he could feel the wetness gathered there. He gave a soft rumble of approval and circled my clit once before delving lower and thrusting two fingers into my core. I cried out and arched into the movement.

"Luca?"

His fingers dipped into me again, his palm pressing deliciously against my mound. "Hmm?"

"Can we skip the buildup this morning?"

"Meaning?" He dragged his fingers out of me, trailed them along the outer lips of my sex, up to the center of my need. He knew damn well what I meant.

"I want your cock in me. Now."

He slid down behind me, until his tip nudged my entrance, pulling my leg over his to grant him better access, and pushed the barest inch inside my channel. Then he stopped. He kissed the back of my neck, that sensitive spot that always sent shivers through me.

"Luca?"

"Yes, my love?" he murmured.

The casual endearment sent flutters through me. "I thought I was pretty clear."

His voice was laced with false surprise. "Have I not done as you asked? My cock, inside you."

"An inch doesn't count."

"No? Perhaps you should have been more specific."

"I'm going to kill you."

"Hmm." He dragged his teeth across my shoulder. "Dying inside you wouldn't be the worst way to go, though I imagine it would be somewhat traumatizing for you."

"If you aren't fully inside me in the next five seconds, I'm going to—"

He flexed his hips and thrust. I closed my eyes and moaned, tilting my hips to deepen his reach.

"Better?" he asked.

"Yes," I said, since he claimed to like the damn word so much. And since morning Luca was apparently playful Luca, and I suspected he could continue this game for an hour if I let him, I decided it was past time to take control of the situation. I shifted until my back was on the mattress and drew my leg wider over his, until my knee cleared his hip and my foot gained purchase on the bed on the other side of him.

Then I shifted my hips and started to ride his cock. It was a favorite position of mine. With Luca on his side, he didn't have much room to move, which meant I controlled everything—the pace, the depth of penetration—even more so than when I was on top, because in that position he could still easily lose patience and drive up into me.

Not so much, now, and I took full advantage, building a rhythm with my hips that took him deep within me. I put my hand between my legs, matching the pace of my hips to the circles I worked on my clit. Luca groaned when I touched myself. His cock throbbed inside me and he reached across to take my breast in his hand, rolling the nipple between his fingers.

I arched into his touch and stroked myself faster, increased the pace so the thick glide of his cock in and out of me was fast and hard.

"You're so fucking beautiful," Luca whispered, squeezing

my breast in a tight grip that had me whimpering and moving on him with frantic urgency. "That's it, baby. Come for me."

My fingers moved in practiced competency and the next surge of my hips, the next hit of him deep inside me, made me shatter. I screamed out his name and came apart, my inner walls clamping down on his cock, spasming around the hard length of him.

"So beautiful," he said again, flipping me onto my stomach so he rose behind me. His fingers traced my spine down to the curves of my ass. He gripped my cheeks in his hands, squeezing and kneading my flesh as he began to fuck me, slowly at first, each lazy thrust thorough and penetrating me to the core. I'd barely recovered from my first orgasm when I felt the next one building.

"Do you have any idea what it does to me to see my dick slide into your sweet pussy? To feel you quiver around me?" His hands settled onto my hips and this time when he thrust into me he pulled me hard against him at the same time, piercing me farther than I'd ever felt before.

I cried out and he rocked his hips in a circle, driving me crazy. I struggled to get my hand between me and the bed, to touch myself, needing a release for the steadily building pressure.

"You're so hot. So willing. So mine." He withdrew and slammed back in. My fingers finally found my aching clit, and I almost came again at the mere touch. "Say you're mine, Ashlynn."

I tried to find words, but they were beyond me. He pulled out and buried himself again. "Say it, Ashlynn. You're mine." There was a growl in his voice, a hint of something feral as he built momentum, thrusting faster and faster, each rough joining of our bodies harder, more urgent, than the last. "Say it," he demanded, with his mouth, his body, with the iron shaft that brought me closer and closer to the precipice. I had this crazy feeling that if I didn't say it, I would never find release again.

"I'm yours," I managed, and my second orgasm tore through me, more potent than the one before as Luca lost himself, pounding into my pussy with feverish abandon. He let out a sound that was all male need and triumph and slammed home a final time, his cock spurting hot and violent as he spent his seed inside me.

He collapsed onto the bed next to me and pulled me to face him, raining kisses on my forehead, my temples, my cheeks. "Good morning," he said with a smile.

I lifted one eyebrow. "If that's how you tell everyone good morning I don't know whether to be concerned or jealous."

"Only for you." He stroked one big hand up my back. "But I like it when you're jealous."

"You *would*." I sighed. Morning sex was great, but now that I could think again, there were a lot of things to do. "Luca, we need to talk."

"Hmm. What we need to do is make breakfast. I haven't eaten since yesterday morning, and I don't think you have, either." He pressed another kiss to my forehead and rolled out of bed, temporarily distracting me with a view of the world's best ass. And the *back* muscles. I just wanted to dig my fingers into them.

He pulled on a pair of sweatpants and exited the room, and my temporarily impaired cognitive function returned. I scrounged for my clothes. Panties: shredded. Bra: serviceable. Jeans and shirt: covered in dirt from last night's forest battle. Ugh. I was going to need to find money to buy clothes sooner rather than later.

I threw the bra on the bed for potential later use and shrugged into one of Luca's T-shirts, rolling the sleeves up. In the kitchen, the blessed smells of coffee and bacon hit me, and I downed half a cup of black coffee before I found my words.

"We need to talk," I said again.

He didn't answer, instead cracking a couple of eggs into a second skillet and monitoring them with the attention of a mother hen, spatula in hand. I'd never have guessed Luca would have learned how to cook, but then I guess self-imposed exile would turn anyone domestic.

"Luca."

He transferred the fried eggs to plates, checked the bacon and pulled the slices out as well. "Can we at least eat breakfast first? Can I have you for a morning before it all goes to hell?"

"Nothing's going to go to hell," I grumbled. But when he pushed a plate at me and gave me a pointed look I caved and said, "Fine. Breakfast. Then talk."

Perhaps because of that stipulation—and also because I *was* starving—I ate in record time. Luca ate as if each bite were a rare delicacy to be savored for a small eternity.

"No one eats that slow. Especially not wolves."

He gave me a look that said, *What? Sorry, can't talk with my mouth full*, and continued to eat with a patience that would have tested even the most virtuous of women, which I wasn't. Not by a long shot.

26

LUCA

I'd never wanted to finish a meal less in my life. In this exact moment, if I ignored the madness happening outside these walls, I had everything I wanted.

Ashlynn Hunter was in my kitchen, in my shirt, and she smelled of me, outside and in. Our scents were so thoroughly intertwined I didn't know if they'd ever separate again and didn't want them to. I wanted every wolf she walked past to know she was completely, unequivocally, *mine*. And if my scent all over her didn't drive them away, the mating bond crackling around her should.

I still couldn't believe that it could be like this, that the bond could just...wait and offer instead of take. I'd never heard of anything like it before. Then again, most of what I'd learned about it had been from hearsay. Aiden Ferrar hadn't precisely been big on conversations about life and love and the intricacies therein. I suspected any softness he'd ever possessed had died with my mother, shortly after I was born.

So I'd had no idea it could be like this. Ash hadn't accepted the bond, but she hadn't pushed it away, either. It stupidly made me imagine the possibility of a future with her and it cut to think that that future might have been possible if it wasn't for the Oracle's damn prophecy. Then again, without that prophecy, she wouldn't be sitting here right now. Thrice again, though, without the *first* prophecy, I'd never have lost her.

When I thought about it like that, my head wanted to explode.

I was down to a single piece of bacon and wondering how long Ash would let me drag that out for when she picked the bacon up, shoved it into my mouth, and clapped her hand over my lips.

"There," she said, sounding entirely too satisfied. "You've eaten breakfast. Talk."

I swallowed and washed the bacon down with a mouthful of coffee. "What did you want to talk about? Ah, wait, let me guess." I propped my elbow on the countertop, rested my chin in my hand, and stared at her with an air of affected concern. "The sex is phenomenal, and you're concerned our future couplings won't be able to compare."

She rolled her eyes. "Luca."

Darkness, I loved it when she said my name. "Fortunately, you inspire no shortage of imagination in me, and I'm happy to demonstrate, immediately, just how creative I can be." I trailed my fingers up her knee to the soft expanse of her thigh. She wore one of my shirts, another thing that made the mating bond very, very happy, and it barely covered her ass. My fingers slipped underneath the hem of the shirt. The sharp tang of her lust hit the air and I thought that maybe I'd get lucky and distract her when she slapped my hand away.

"Be serious." A smile she fought very hard to quell tugged at the edges of her lips.

"Oh, I'm always serious about two things, love. Sex, and you."

"Try being serious about prophecy for a minute."

I grimaced. "I thought you weren't interested in prophecy and the Darkness."

"I've rethought my position."

"Rethink it again in the other direction."

She threw up her hands—good to know I could still irritate her to distraction—and demanded, "Why?"

"Because you won't like the answer."

"Wouldn't be the first time."

I took her hand. If she insisted on going down this road, it was probably the last time she would let me touch her. Couldn't she have waited *one* day? But Ashlynn Hunter didn't wait. For anything. Once she got something into her head she ran with it, like a bull on a rampage, until she either destroyed everything in her path or ran out of energy.

I turned her hand over, pulled it to my lips and pressed a kiss to her palm. "Please don't ask."

"*Why?*"

"Because I don't want to lose you."

She drew back—not much, and she didn't take her hand from mine—but it still hurt.

"Why would you?"

I didn't answer. It seemed the safest option.

"You don't want to talk? Fine. I will. I'm going to tell you what I know, and when I'm done, if you haven't filled in the gaps, I am going to go out there" —she pointed out the door — "and I'm going to find someone who will.

"So here's what I know. First, you really wanted me to come home. You went on and on about the Darkness and the dangers to Elysium and how I needed to come home and fix them.

"Now that I'm here, no one wants me to do anything. No one wants to *tell* me anything. No one wants to tell me what the prophecy says, or give me any actually useful information, or let me have my Heartstone back, or *anything*.

"In fact, the only thing anyone seems interested in *at all* is whether or not you and I are together and—" She snapped her mouth shut, and I saw the pieces clicking together for her. She narrowed her eyes, carefully pulled her hand out of mine, and spoke again in an all-too-measured tone. "Luca. Is there something in this prophecy about you and me?"

I wanted to lie to her, but I gritted out, "Yes."

"Something about us being together?"

"Yes."

"What the fuck does the prophecy *say?*"

There was no getting around it. There never had been. I walked around the kitchen counter, opened one of the drawers, and pulled out the copy of the prophecy I'd written down when I was hoping there was some way—any way—to convince the Elders it didn't mean what they thought it meant. At least with regard to the Heartstone clause. But the damn thing was pretty clear.

I put the paper facedown on the countertop, held it pinned with my fingers when Ash reached for it.

"Before you read it, you should know two things. One, I don't believe in this bullshit any more than you do."

"And two?"

"Nothing I've done with you has been about this in any way." I willed her to believe it as I lifted my fingers and let her take the page, but I didn't know if she would. Didn't know if it would matter if she did.

I didn't need to read along with her to know every word— I'd memorized the damn thing trying to find a loophole in it, but it wasn't prophecy of the sort that was difficult to inter-pret. It was more like bad poetry that had enough contingent clauses that the Oracle could throw up his hands and point to any condition that hadn't been met if the Six failed to solve the problem of the Darkness.

I watched Ash's face, repeated the words in my head as she read.

> *Though we have seen the Darkness grow,*
> *What was done before was not in vain,*
> *The Six cast out must now return,*
> *To vanquish evil from this land.*
>
> *To find them in the mortal realm,*
> *For each of the Six, a destined mate,*
> *To anchor them to Elysium*
> *And stand beside them in their trials.*
>
> *Each of the Six must accept her Fate,*
> *In body and soul,*
> *In Heart and mind,*
> *Each must join with the one who is hers.*
>
> *The Heart taken from each may be returned*
> *But only to be given again in half*
> *Only with Hearts broken and reforged*
> *Will the Six have the strength to conquer the Darkness.*
>
> *Only when all have returned*
> *Shall the prophecy be fulfilled*
> *Only through the Six's power combined*
> *Will Elysium be made whole again.*
>
> *And those who share Hearts*
> *Who have battled great Darkness*
> *Shall take the mantle of those who came before*
> *And lead Elysium into the next era.*

She finished and shoved the paper away from her in disgust. "What the bloody fuck?" She demanded. "Has the Oracle been getting high and reading mortal paranormal romance? Destined mates? Are you fucking kidding me?"

She kept ranting and I let her, because right now she was cursing in general and not specifically at me. She seemed to realize that herself and rectified the shortcoming when she came to the end of a sentence particularly rich with four-letter words and rounded on me.

"You." She stabbed a finger at me. "You aren't mentioned in this."

"The Elders thought the people needed a show." My lip curled up in distaste. "They made a big production out of having the Oracle announce the first of the Six who would come home, and which of us was going to go find her."

"And he named *you* for me? And you just went along with it?"

She hadn't thrown anything at me yet. I considered it a cautious cause for optimism.

"No, I didn't just *go along with it*. The night before the Oracle made the announcement I broke into his home, put my claws to his throat and told him when it came your turn, he wasn't going to name anyone but me."

That stunned her. "You did *what*?"

"I had a promise to keep. And I might have been twelve years late in keeping it, but I damn well did."

"And the Oracle just...agreed?" The incredulity was painted on her face.

"He didn't have to. He'd already written my name next to yours." I shook my head. "In retrospect, it makes sense. Everyone on the island knows we were inseparable as kids, knows I went berserk when you left. Damn Oracle couldn't have picked a better story to start off with. Childhood friends, destined to grow up and fall in love. Everybody thought it, even before any of the prophecy mess started."

I wished I knew what she was thinking. Wished she would yell at me, really yell, so we could get this over with and I could know if she hated me, or if I still had some sliver of a chance.

She pushed off her chair and started pacing. "And your fight with Aiden yesterday? This fucking mess with Clay?"

I clenched my teeth. Unclenched them. "I was under the alpha's strictest orders to force a bond on you the moment I found you. I told him to go fuck himself but apparently he didn't think I meant it. He's determined to have the White Woods pack bound to the prophecy at any cost. He said if I didn't force the bond, someone else would."

She stopped pacing and her voice went dangerously soft. "And you didn't think that was information I needed to fucking have?"

"I told you not to trust the pack."

"Telling me not to trust the pack is worlds away from 'random wolves may try to mate with you'."

"I *told* you to fucking wait for me at the castle."

"You should have told me the goddamn truth," she shouted.

"I know," I whispered.

She took the admission and seemed to turn it over in her head, looking for a hidden trap. "Then why didn't you?" she finally asked.

"You've read the damn prophecy. You get what the last lines mean?"

"I get that the Oracle's cracked in the head if he thinks the Elders are going to step aside and let Six exiled women replace them. I'm surprised they even let that part of the prophecy go public."

"They didn't have much of a choice. He made it in the middle of the High Solstice Festival."

She gaped. "The *Oracle* went to the High Solstice Festival?"

I nodded. "And by 'in the middle of' I mean he wandered in during the big speech, crazy hair and tattered robe and everything, rattled it off, and collapsed in the street."

"Why does anyone believe anything he says? He's obviously crazy."

"Good question." The better one was, why did the *Elders* believe everything he said?

She looked like she was seconds away from ripping her hair out. Or mine. Knowing Ash, probably mine.

"What does the Oracle wanting to upset the chain of command have to do with you not telling me about the prophecy?"

"Everyone on this damn island believes *you* are going to be one of the next Elders. But not just you. Whoever stands at your side. Whoever you give half your Heartstone to. Right now, I'm the *only* protection you have from the hordes descending on you en masse.

"And I *know you*, Ashlynn. If I'd told you the Oracle put us together you would have run as far away from me as you could."

Her silence, her brief turn away from me, was confirmation enough that I'd been right on that.

"If you publicly denounced me," I continued, "people would line up around the island to try and take you. There wouldn't just be one Clay, there would be hundreds." She shivered a little, hid it quickly, and I decided right then and there I was never saying that bastard's name in front of her again.

"But the Oracle named you."

"Yes. But not in prophecy. The Heartstone is what's in the prophecy, Ash. And you might have to be the one to break yours, but there are a lot of people who wouldn't be above forcing you to do it."

"And that's why you didn't tell me? To protect me? That's the *only* reason?"

"No." I swallowed, hard. "It started out as the only reason. It didn't stay that way for long."

She slipped around the kitchen counter and stopped a foot away from me. "What's the other reason, Luca?"

"Do you really need me to tell you?"

"Yes. I really do."

"I wanted you. If there was a chance you wanted me at all, I didn't want you to turn your back on it because of this stupid prophecy."

"Is that what you think I'll do? Leave?"

"I'm surprised you haven't already."

That might have been the wrong thing to say. She looked more than a little pissed off. "You think I'm that fickle?"

"You told me you had no intention of, and I quote, 'playing the Prophesied Savior of Elysium.' That the second you didn't like what you saw, you'd leave."

She bit her lip and looked away. "I did say that."

An erratic feeling I dared not classify as hope stuttered through me. "Don't tell me you've changed your mind."

"About believing in prophecy? No."

"If you're going to leave me, Ash, just do it."

She pondered it. "Luca, the only thing dumber than tying myself to you for the rest of my life because a prophecy told me to, would be leaving the man I love to spite a prophecy that claims I should be with him."

"What?" My head spun. I was pretty sure I'd heard a four-letter word that started with L but I couldn't be sure.

"If the prophecy doesn't mean anything, it doesn't mean anything. I'm not going to let it dictate what I do."

"I meant *what* to the other thing you said," I whispered, hoarsely.

"Oh." She smiled a little, closed the last foot of distance between us, and looked up at me. "I love you, Luca Ferrar. I always have."

27

ASHLYNN

For the rest of my life, I would remember the look that spread across Luca's face when I told him I loved him. It was a mix of stunned wonder, confusion, and terrified joy. For five whole seconds he just stood there. Then he exploded into action and yanked me to him, his lips meeting mine, tongue thrusting between my teeth.

My hands twined in his hair. I jumped onto his hips, locked my legs around his waist, and met him stroke for stroke.

"You should say that again," he said between kisses, "when I'm inside you."

He was already hard and ready, and my body responded to him, my core going wet and molten as if on command. But I needed to know one other thing, first.

"Luca." I splayed my hands across his chest, gently holding him back from devouring me like he clearly wanted to. "Where *is* my Heartstone?"

He stilled and set me down on the counter. I kept my legs around him, refusing to let him retreat.

"Do you have it?" I asked.

"Yes."

"Show me." I held my breath. If he said *no*, if he refused…

The air shimmered with the tear of glamour being ripped away. But it wasn't just the glamour over *his* Heartstone that disappeared. It was the glamour over mine, dangling from a chain around his neck. It had been right in front of me the whole time and I hadn't known, hadn't seen it, hadn't realized — "Holy shit," I whispered.

Because my Heartstone wasn't *only* my Heartstone. There, melded to it, was half of Luca's. I remembered Luca's power pouring into my wrist, the certainty that it was his werewolf healing abilities closing the wound over. Something that shouldn't have been possible.

I didn't know of anyone living who had actually done this, actually given part of their Heartstone to another. But the legends said that if someone did, the person they gave it to could share their power.

"You can't undo this." Even if I wanted to give it back to him, a Heartstone, once given, could never be returned. It was precisely *why* no one did it. "Why? *When?*"

"Before I left to find you. Because I knew you wouldn't want anything to do with this, and it was the only assurance I could give the Elders, the only thing I could do to buy you some time."

I couldn't speak, couldn't move, not even to reach out and touch my Heartstone, pulsing so near and *mine*. Luca's worried eyes looked into mine. He reached up to cup my face in his hands, thumbs stroking across my cheekbones.

"Say something."

"You gave half your Heartstone to mine to *buy me some time?*" The scale of the sacrifice for the reward was absurd. It was like a soldier throwing herself across enemy lines to buy her comrades five seconds when those five seconds wouldn't make any difference in the outcome. "Are you crazy?"

"Most of the island thinks so." He smiled as he said it, actually *smiled*, like it was the punchline of a hilarious joke.

"*Luca*. What were you buying me time for?"

The smile faded. "The Elders were very clear when they gave this to me." He tapped my Heartstone. "If you don't join it with mine of your own volition, they have every intention of forcing you to."

"They *what*?" I shouldn't be surprised. I wasn't, really. But pissed? Oh, yeah. I was that.

"I won't let that happen, Ash. And if you ask me to give this back to you, I will. But while I still have it, they think I'm committed to getting you to do what they want. We can use that time. If we can claim an actual victory over the Darkness, if we can prove to people it can be fought without this stupid prophecy, they won't be able to make you do this."

I thought he had a naively optimistic belief about the Elders bowing to peer pressure. And none of that changed one simple fact. "Even if that's true, even if it works, you've literally chained yourself to me, Luca. Forever." Was he going to hate me for that some day?

He smiled. "I've been chained for you before."

I gave him my best you-did-not-just-say-that look.

"And there was never any separating from you. Not for me. Whether you want me or don't, my heart's yours. I love you, Ashlynn Hunter. I always have."

This whole situation—Heartstone, prophecy, Darkness, Elders—was a fucking mess. But Luca telling me he loved me? Giving my own words back to me? Knowing he meant them? That was perfect. And I could delay the mess for another hour of perfect.

"You should say that again," I said, rising up to kiss him, "when you're inside me."

He'd just let out one of those pleased male growls and slid his hands beneath my shirt when someone pounded on the door. When we didn't answer they pounded again, more insistent this time.

Luca's growl turned annoyed. I nipped at his neck. "Go be princely and tell them to fuck off."

"Stay right here," he ordered.

I jumped off the counter, both because I'd never done well with ultimatums, and because I didn't want to flash whoever had come calling.

Luca wrenched the door open. He didn't manage a single syllable before Gareth breezed in carrying a bag. He made it a whole two steps inside before he made fake choking noises and waved his hand frantically in front of his face. "For Darkness sake open a window. If this place smells any more like sex spontaneous orgasms are going to start happening."

"No one invited you to the party," I pointed out.

He clapped a hand to his chest. "And I'm wounded, truly."

I gave him a casual once-over. "I don't think we're accepting applicants for a threesome right now, but I'll keep you at the top of the list if the mood ever strikes."

"Really?"

"No," Luca answered, coming over to snake a possessive arm around my waist and pull me against him.

Gareth rolled his eyes. "You're no fun. Congratulations, by the way, it's about damn time."

"I've been back for all of a day and a half. Was I supposed to climb on top of him the second I laid eyes on him?"

"I think that was the general consensus, yes."

"Gareth, what are you doing here?" Luca asked.

"Well, since you were too busy fucking her brains out to think about anything practical, I brought her some clothes."

Thank God. "Ooh, give." I extricated myself from Luca, who reluctantly let me go, and held out my hands. Gareth deposited the bag in them and I tore it open. Pants. Shirts.

Socks. Boots. Even the underwear and bras looked like they would fit, right down to the cup size.

A fact that apparently wasn't lost on Luca. "Did the tailor measure her when I wasn't looking?"

Gareth grinned. "What sort of wolf would I be if I couldn't accurately guess a woman's clothing size?"

"The kind no one's ever heard a whisper of having an affair. Including his best friend."

Gareth's grin faltered, shadows darkening his eyes. He shrugged. "Some of us know how to be discreet." He said it lightly, but there was a trace of some old hurt in his voice, the sentence a slight dig at Luca. Which was odd, because wolves, as a general rule, *weren't* discreet. It took an enormous amount of effort to be so, considering how much scrubbing and showering someone would have to do after a tryst to make sure wolves couldn't smell their partner on them.

Gareth's annoyance at Luca's lack of discretion added up to one thing: Gareth had it bad for someone in the pack, and that someone had slept with Luca. Jealousy and curiosity warred within me. On the one hand, I really didn't need a laundry list of Luca's ex-lovers. Knowing he'd slept with Kiera was bad enough—I didn't need the rest of the pack's beauties trotted out for me to compare myself to.

They were in the past. Luca didn't want them now, he wanted *me*, and that was all that mattered.

On the other hand, I really, really wanted to know who Gareth was pining over. He looked like a kicked puppy right now, and Luca was completely oblivious.

It was beyond me to not fix a sad Gareth, and there was only one thing that could break a man out of that deep a level moroseness. I walked up to him, framed his face in my hands, and kissed him dead on the mouth.

"Thank you, Gareth, for thinking of me. I'm going to go

try these on." I grabbed the bag and headed toward Luca's bedroom, leaving two very stunned wolves in my wake.

Gareth recovered first. "I can think of you more often, if that's the thanks I get," he called after me.

"You," Luca growled, "outside. Let's talk."

I kicked the door to Luca's bedroom shut, surveyed my clothing options, and decided since I actually had clean clothes that weren't stiff with saltwater, sweat, dirt, or blood, I should probably be clean as well before I put them on. Luca would probably be half an hour growling at Gareth anyway. I might as well shower.

❦ 28 ❦

LUCA

"ALL RIGHT," I SAID, ONCE THE DOOR BETWEEN US AND ASH was closed, "talk."

Gareth lifted an eyebrow. "Not even going to take a token swing at me over that kiss?"

"No." Truth was, I was grateful to Ash for snapping Gareth back to reality. He had been...off. For about a year now. There had been six months where I'd hardly seen him. Considering he was the only member of the pack I knew didn't have an ulterior motive for spending time with me, it had hit hard.

His absence was why I'd let Kiera stay in my bed longer than I should have. Fortunately, Gareth had come somewhat back to himself a few weeks after I broke it off with her, but he still wasn't...normal. Wasn't the easygoing Gareth I'd always known.

He could go from laughing to moody to a hairs breadth away from sprouting fur and claws in the span of a second. Considering what I knew about where he fit in the pack hierarchy, an angry Gareth was an extremely dangerous one.

Everyone assumed he ranked low, because he'd refused to

fight after we hit adolescence. And that refusal stemmed from the first time he and I had ever seriously locked claws. Gareth wasn't at the bottom of the pack, or the middle. He was at the bloody pinnacle and neither of us knew which one of us would come out on top in a fight.

Without ever giving me a say in the matter, Gareth had decided he was going to remove himself from the pack hierarchy entirely, so it never became an issue. He'd taken a ripping for it for a few years, but he was easygoing and funny and everyone liked him. Considering that I would also remove myself from the damn pack hierarchy if I could, I couldn't blame him for his choice.

He'd always been happy with it. Which was why it was so damn odd that I would swear there had been times in the last year when he'd looked at me like he wanted to rip my throat out. I'd sat him down one night, gotten him dead drunk, and asked him what the hell I'd done to him.

He'd just shaken his head, said it was nothing he could blame me for, and then I hadn't seen him again for two weeks.

"Why are you really here, Gareth?" If he'd wanted to bring Ash clothes he could have left them on the damn doorstep.

"Clay."

"What the fuck about him?"

"You ripped him apart and left his body in the woods."

"He tried to force a fucking mating bond on her. He tried to force *her*. I'm entirely within the rights of pack law."

"*I* get that. Unfortunately, she left with him more or less willingly and he used his one brain cell to be smart enough not to try anything until they were out of hearing range. Evan's saying you went on a jealous rampage."

Clay's brother could say whatever the fuck he wanted. "Why do I care? It's not like I was winning any fucking popularity contests before this mess."

"Evan called for a pack trial. Tonight." The long silence that followed told me everything.

"And my father granted it," I guessed. Gareth nodded. My father, the pack alpha, had just given me a public vote of no-confidence. "Son of a bitch."

"He wants one of the Six tied to White Woods. Way I figure it, he thinks this will go one of two ways. One, the trial convicts you, the entire pack tries to kill you, and he's then free to force a bond on her, or two, you panic and do it. Either way, he wins."

"I'll never force her."

"I know." He hesitated. "Things looked like they were going good in there. She obviously knows everything now." He nodded at her now-visible Heartstone hanging around my neck. "If you asked her, would she take the bond?"

My blood boiled at the very mention. Half in disgust, and half in longing for that exact outcome. "I'm not going to ask her. Not after what Clay tried to do to her, not under these circumstances."

"It would fix everything."

I knew what I'd do, then, knew what I *had* to do. "*I* will fix everything. Stay here and make sure nothing happens to her."

"Where are you going?"

"To do what I should have done twelve years ago."

Gareth's eyes widened. "You're going to—"

"Nothing. Happens. To her." I repeated. "No one hurts her, no one *touches* her. Am I clear?"

Gareth nodded once, short and sharp. "Yes, Alpha."

And damn if I didn't already hate the sound of that title.

❦ 29 ❦

ASHLYNN

I'D JUST RINSED THE CONDITIONER OUT OF MY HAIR—Elysians had been on to solid shampoo and conditioner bars way before environmentally-conscious mortals—when a knock sounded on the bathroom door.

"Since when do you knock?" I called. Frankly, I'd drawn out the shower longer than necessary hoping Luca would come interrupt me during it. I bet he was great at shower sex. All those muscles, all that balance. He could hold me against the wall, drive into me, and—

"Since my alpha would probably kill me if I saw you naked," Gareth answered. "And *please* stop thinking whatever the hell you were thinking when you thought I was Luca. That much lust is distracting to delicate noses."

I turned the water to freezing cold for a good ten seconds and shut it off. "Gareth, where the hell is Luca?"

"He had something to go take care of. I'm supposed to make sure nothing happens to you in the interim."

I furiously dried off, wrapped the towel around me and yanked open the door. "Where did he go?"

"Geez, Hunter, clothes."

"Talk."

"Clothes first," he insisted. "The pair of you are a couple of hotheads and when you inevitably go bursting out of this house, I'd prefer it wasn't bare-ass naked."

"Fine." I stormed past him, trying to ignore the worry building in my stomach, since I was pretty sure nothing good would have dragged Luca away from me without so much as a word from him. Gareth kept his back to me while I threw on the necessities—he really was scary good at guessing sizes—and started strapping on weaponry. "Clothed. Where is he?"

Gareth turned around, apparently needing to confirm the "clothed" part, and prevaricated. "Pack business."

"Luca lives in a cabin that can just barely be considered in White Woods territory. He got chained to a fucking tree while nobody did a goddamn thing about it. What pack business am I supposed to believe he suddenly gives a fuck about?"

"Something long overdue?" he offered.

My brain rewound a few clicks to the very first thing Gareth had said after he'd knocked on the bathroom door. He'd said his *alpha would kill him for seeing me naked*. I remembered Luca's casual certainty that morning when he'd said he should have challenged Aiden a long time ago: *I could have replaced Aiden when I was fourteen.*

"He's challenging for leadership?"

"I mean, he didn't say so in as many words—"

"*Why?*"

Succinctly, he explained the situation with Clay.

"Fuck." I threw my boots on, laced them, and sprinted for the door.

"Couple of damn hotheads," Gareth muttered and bounded after me.

"Why are you being so calm?" I demanded. "Your best friend's about to get himself killed."

"He's not going to get himself killed."

I broke into a jog as we hit the woods. Of course Luca was going to get himself killed. Aiden was a big, scary asshole who didn't care about anyone. Why wasn't Gareth concerned? "Is this lack of concern because of whoever Luca slept with that you're obviously in love with?"

If it hadn't been for the long pause before he said, "I don't know what you're talking about," I might have believed him.

"Sure you don't. Look, I definitely don't want to know who all Luca's slept with in my absence, but who are you hung up on? The only person I know he's been with is Kiera and—"

Gareth tripped over a root.

I didn't quit running, because I needed to get to my lover before he got his stupid ass killed, but I did look back over my shoulder to see the stricken, tortured look on Gareth's face before he covered it.

"*Kiera?*" I said. "You're in love with *Kiera?*"

"Could you maybe not say that so fucking loud?" he whisper-shouted at me. "Wolf ears are everywhere."

If Luca was challenging Aiden, I could guaran-fucking-tee that all wolf ears were currently at the pack clearing. "Why the hell didn't you say something to him?"

For a moment, I thought he wasn't going to answer. Finally, he said, "Because it doesn't matter. She doesn't want me. She wants the next pack alpha. I'm not going to stand in the way of her fucking ambitions."

"In case you forgot, Luca's *mine*. You're not the one standing in the way of her ambitions. I am."

"It's complicated," Gareth said.

"Isn't everything? I'm running to stop my supposedly-destined mate from getting his dumb ass killed and trying to figure out what to do about mating bonds and Heartstones and all you have to do is tell a pretty girl you like her."

"Ash?"

"Yes?"

"Shut up."

Ouch. "Fine. But we're talking about this later."

I let him have his damn silence. We were almost to the clearing when I heard the snapping, snarling sounds of fighting wolves. *Shit.* I was too late to stop it from happening.

How was I too late? Had Aiden been sitting in the fucking clearing with the rest of the pack in attendance waiting for Luca to come challenge him?

Yes, I decided, that was probably *exactly* what he'd been doing. He'd wanted his son out of the way, so he'd engineered a scenario guaranteed to make Luca challenge him.

I put on an extra burst of speed and we came out at the clearing's edge. In the center of the ring formed by pack members, Luca and Aiden fought.

Luca's white fur was pink and red with blood, and I had no idea how much of it was his and how much was Aiden's. The dark brown wolf that was the current pack alpha circled Luca, growling and snapping.

I wondered how many times they'd grappled and nearly ended each other. With werewolf healing, I had no way of knowing. Challenges could last far longer than any ordinary fight, until one party was injured enough they exhausted the reserves of their magic and couldn't heal anymore.

Or until one party yielded by shifting to human. That almost never happened. If a wolf was willing to challenge, he was willing to die.

I tensed as Aiden dove for an opening on Luca's flank, relaxed slightly when Luca pivoted and knocked him aside. I repeated this cycle several times, tensing and relaxing every time Aiden made a move, until I finally realized why Gareth was watching it all with an air of bored nonchalance.

Luca and Aiden might be near-matched in strength, but Luca was clearly the better fighter. The last time I'd seen

Aiden fight, *really* fight, I'd been a kid. To my child's eyes, Aiden had been larger, and brutal, and unstoppable.

He was *still* large and brutal, but he wasn't unstoppable. Luca *was*. He was fast and canny and moved with a nimbleness one wouldn't expect from a wolf his size. And the way he fended off attacks with ease, darting in to score wounds that would have been fatal to non-wolves, I thought this fight should have already been over.

"Is Luca *toying* with him?" I hissed at Gareth. The wolves around me had to have heard me—I didn't have their talent for talking at near subvocal volumes—but no one said anything. No one took their eyes off the fight.

"He's making a point," Gareth said, and he didn't even pretend to try and be quiet, apparently one-hundred percent confident in the soon-to-be-changed leadership of the pack. "That he isn't winning this fight by luck. And he's also trying to make Aiden realize he's outmatched so he has the chance to yield. Aiden may be a bastard but Luca's not *wanting* to kill his own father."

I almost replied that Aiden Ferrar wouldn't yield in a million years when the very thing happened. Furry bodies clashed. The sound of Aiden's foreleg breaking cracked through the air and in the resultant tumble Luca pinned him to the ground, teeth clamped around Aiden's throat, claws raking across his belly.

And Aiden Ferrar shed fur and fang and turned human.

The silence took on a different quality now. Stunned. Waiting.

Luca could still kill him. A yield didn't guarantee your life. Part of me wanted Luca to do it. To end it so we never had to worry about Aiden again. Because I didn't trust him, didn't trust that this wasn't a ploy of some type.

Luca clearly had his own reservations. He removed his teeth from Aiden's throat but kept him pinned. Verbal acknowledgment wasn't necessary for a yield—going human was all that was—but it *felt* necessary.

Instead of triumph, a leaden sense of dread grew in my gut. Even as I tried to quell it, told myself I was being paranoid, I saw the glint of silver. I didn't see who threw the knife. But it went straight to Aiden's good hand, quick as a flash, and he plunged the silver dagger into Luca's chest.

The scream that left me wasn't human, wasn't even close. I launched myself into the ring made of pack members—pack who weren't doing a damn thing in response to Aiden yielding a challenge and then sinking a blade into the pack's new alpha. Gareth was the only one who tried to move to him and Kiera—fucking *Kiera*—appeared out of nowhere and held him back, saying something low and urgent to him I couldn't make out and didn't care to try.

All I cared about was Luca, was *getting* to Luca. Aiden shoved Luca off him, then rose to his knees but not any farther. Though his wounds weren't openly bleeding, he had the wan look of a man who'd lost too much blood.

I sprinted toward Luca, nothing but rage and fury left in me. The mating bond, which had clung to me like a second skin since the moment Luca let it out, flickered and wavered.

No. It couldn't disappear, because if it did, it meant Luca was dead.

I grabbed hold of the bond with mental fingers and awareness slammed through me at the voluntary touch: Luca's pain, the tip of the silver blade just piercing his heart. His fear, not for himself, but for me, for what would become of me if he wasn't here. The panic rose when he saw me running toward him and he tried to scrabble to his feet.

Aiden's head came up, focusing on his son.

No, you idiot, stay down. But Luca couldn't hear my mental thoughts. Because he wasn't mine in the way of wolves.

Because we weren't mated. And as he kept struggling to rise, Aiden did too.

I charged Aiden like a bull, barreling into him, and as I bore him to the ground, my fist connecting with his face with all the force of my own fear and fury behind it, I took the mating bond Luca offered and welcomed it into me.

It slipped through my skin like fog through a screen, every empty, lonely place inside me suddenly filled with *Luca*. With his presence, his magic, his love.

His shock at my acceptance rippled through me, and underneath it I felt what he tried to keep from me but couldn't anymore, because we were mated now, because he was *mine*: his pain.

The silver of the dagger burned, a central point of acid-dipped agony from which fire radiated. The tip pierced his heart, not deep enough for that instant kill, just deep enough that all his healing abilities focused on it, trying over and over to close the wound around the still-embedded blade. And the magic that tried was almost spent.

He needed the blade removed but the silver kept him from shifting to the human form that would have allowed him to do so.

Hold on, I ordered, and the command thundered through the bond, my need for him to *live* given weight and tangibility. I sank a punch to Aiden's throat, crushing his windpipe. It would heal, but Luca had worn him down enough that it wouldn't be fast. I stood and brought my foot down on Aiden's half-healed broken arm, hearing the satisfying crunch of a fresh break.

Then I ran to Luca. I dropped to my knees at his side, braced one hand on his massive shoulder, gripped the hilt of the knife with the other, and ripped the blade free.

Aiden gained his feet, his snarl echoing through the clearing, and launched himself at us. I turned in one fluid motion, silver knife in hand, judging angle and trajectory with a Hunter's precision. And when Aiden impaled himself on the blade, when it slipped past his ribs and to his heart and I *twisted*, it was the instant kill he'd failed to achieve with Luca.

The soft whine Luca let out wasn't audible. It traveled down the mating bond, only to me, *for* me.

It's okay, I sent back, settling at his side. *You're going to be fine.*

He wasn't going to be fine. Blood gushed from the wound where I'd removed the knife. The wound that wasn't healing over, the wound the bond told me *wouldn't* heal over because Luca didn't have enough left.

You always were a shitty liar, Ash. Even his mental voice was weak, a soft whisper that said he was fading, fading, and there was nothing I could do to stop it.

I pressed my hand against his chest, trying to stop the flow of blood, willing my own magic to leave me, to go to him. But it didn't. The mating bond didn't allow for that kind of transference.

I love you, he whispered in my mind. But he wasn't saying *I love you*. The son of a bitch was saying *goodbye*.

No. He didn't *get* to say goodbye. He didn't get to leave. My fingertips brushed the cool edges of his Heartstone. He'd given *me* his magic when I'd needed it. Because of this. Because of the half of his Heartstone melded to mine.

I didn't have to think. It wasn't a decision that even needed to be made. Fuck prophecy and everyone's opinions. I didn't care if I played right into their expectations. Because a life without Luca wasn't one I wanted to live.

My fingers found my Heartstone, grasped it in both hands. Before I could even try to break it by physical means, it came apart, responding to my will alone. The half of Luca's Heartstone that had sat atop mine before slid neatly down as the half of mine below it cleaved from the whole, his Heart and mine fusing together into a perfect, smooth disk, half blue, half amber.

I cradled my new Heart in one hand, the broken half of my old Heart in the other. Hands shaking, I felt along Luca's chest, through blood and fur for the edge of his Heartstone, and pressed the lone half of mine to it. The edges pulled together, sealed.

If accepting the mating bond had given me an awareness of Luca, that awareness had still been filtered through a different lens. I had felt it as pain, but it had still been *his* pain. With half my Heartstone in his chest it was *my* pain, *ours*.

My strength, my magic, poured into him. And though my power wasn't a werewolf's healing ability, once it left me and flowed into Luca, the distinction didn't matter. His Heartstone—His? Mine? Ours?—took what I offered and made it his. His power, his ability.

The wound in his chest stopped bleeding and healed over, the pain receding, lifting. The fog that had settled over his mind cleared, an astonished wonder in its place. Magic ripped the air and Luca shifted, fur and fangs melting as his lupine form became human.

He rolled to his feet and brought me with him. It wasn't until his gaze moved around us, assessing, that I remembered we weren't alone. Remembered where we were, what I'd *done*.

Shit. I'd just killed the White Woods alpha.

Or had I? Aiden had yielded to Luca, so technically, hadn't Luca been the alpha when I killed Aiden? Or was there something more official needed for a full transfer of authority? Would the technicalities of it even matter to the pack?

The tension and readiness of Luca's stance told me he would have already shoved me behind him if it weren't for the fact we were in the middle of a living circle so the action wouldn't provide any protection.

Gareth broke from the line of that circle, dropped to one knee, and inclined his head. "Alphas," he said.

My brain screeched to a halt. Had he just said *Alphas*? As in, plural?

The pack had the same reaction, the clearing drowning in a cacophony of angry voices.

Through it all, one voice cut through the rest, clear and commanding. "Quiet," Luca ordered. The command wasn't just verbal, it was magical, tied to a thread that ran from Luca through the entire pack, with Luca at the pinnacle of that connection. Luca...and me.

My place in that web of magical pack connections was less certain. I had become pack when I accepted Luca's mating bond, that acceptance the only thing that could tie a non-werewolf into the magic that bound the pack. But though an alpha's mate enjoyed many privileges within pack society, they weren't considered a part of its leadership.

Yet pack magic had placed me there, at the apex, tied at the head of the hierarchy alongside Luca. The bond that held me there was less certain. As if the magic wasn't quite sure whether I belonged their or not.

In the void of silence that followed Luca's order, support came from the least expected of places. Kiera Silvermoon stepped forward.

"Aiden yielded to Luca. That makes Luca alpha. But Aiden also refused to surrender the alpha's magic. Ash killed him when he still held those reins. That makes her alpha, too," Kiera finished. She dropped to one knee next to Gareth, and the bond that tethered me to alpha status glowed just a little bit brighter at her affirmation.

If it weren't for the fact I was standing in a literal circle of hungry wolves I would have pinched myself to make sure I wasn't dreaming. Of all the wolves present, Kiera had the least reason to support me. She was my mate's former lover and she'd made no secret of wanting to be where I was right now.

Hell, she'd thrown a damn knife at my head less than twenty-four hours ago.

I met her gaze and she lifted her chin slightly, her eyes ablaze, as if daring me to challenge her support. What the hell? I didn't understand it, I didn't entirely trust it, but her gaze held a kind of honest brutality I found difficult to disbelieve.

I was under no illusion that she liked me. I didn't think we were in danger of suddenly becoming besties. But she'd chosen to back me up, to back Luca up. And when this was over, I was going to find out why. If for no other reason than so I could discharge the debt I felt opening up between us.

Slowly, one by one, the rest of the pack took a knee with muttered acknowledgments of, "Alphas." With each bent knee, my position within the pack deepened, solidified, until I knew, because the pack knew, that I *was alpha*.

Even if one knee had yet to bend. Brogan Silvermoon, Aiden's beta, stood tall and unyielding, his eyes boring holes into his daughter, the slow simmer of anger rippling beneath the lines of his body.

"If you have a problem being our beta, Brogan, the time to abdicate is now." Luca's voice was quiet and deceptively calm.

What happens if he doesn't abdicate? I asked Luca privately, words traveling down the mating bond between us.

Then we're stuck with him until someone challenges him for the position.

You can't just remove him?

I could, Luca said reluctantly. *But he has a lot of support within the pack. I'll end up having to kill him. It will be messy. We'll spend the next year fighting challenges every damn week.*

We were going to have to rewrite the laws of challenge if a

human was going to be alpha. They were required to happen in wolf form, but I didn't have one.

As if the thought had woken my Heartstone it flushed with heat, still gripped tight in the palm of my hand. Magic flowed from me, through it to Luca, and back. As it did, I felt that magic shift and change, and as it flowed back into me, it brought with it something wild and foreign. Something *wolf*.

My fingertips lengthened, stretching into claws, glossy brown fur sprouting along the backs of my hands, spreading up my arms.

Luca? I couldn't keep the panic, the terror, out of my mental voice as magic snapped around me, as I fell to all fours and my body *shifted*, bones and muscles and tendons shortening or lengthening, organs moving place inside me.

My vision changed, sharpened, and I looked down—at my *paws*.

Holy shit, was Luca's very helpful reply. *You're a wolf.* There was wonder in his voice, amazement, and—happiness.

Is this fucking normal, Luca? I had never once, in the entirety of my life, expected to find myself with a tail and four paws, and it was freaking me the fuck out just a little. *Does this happen to every human mated to a wolf?*

But I knew the answer, even before he said, *It's the Heartstones, Ash.*

I didn't know if this had happened because it was always *going* to happen after we merged our Heartstones, or if it had been a result of my wayward thought about how pack challenges to a human alpha would work. Either way, I was a fucking *werewolf* now.

I wasn't sure how I felt about it, but I did know what I was going to do with it. I turned on Brogan Silvermoon, bared my teeth in a wide, wolf grin, and snarled. Brogan snarled back.

If you want to challenge me, I told him, my voice broadcasting to everyone through the pack bonds, *I'm more than happy to accept.*

"*We* are happy to accept," Luca corrected, one hand settling on my shoulder, making it clear that challenging *me* was challenging Luca.

Brogan surveyed Luca, then the pack, and realized he didn't have any allies in the latter. At least none that would come forward right now. Most of the hostility I'd felt through the pack bonds had vanished the second I'd sprouted fur.

Brogan's animosity only grew. He took a knee, but every line of his body shouted defiance. "No challenge, Alphas. I'm happy to serve as your beta."

Which was the closest thing to a public "fuck you" he could offer us. He'd tried to bring Luca to trial. He'd probably known what his son was going to try with me. I would put money on him being the one who'd supplied Aiden with the silver dagger that had almost ended Luca's life.

Brogan didn't respect either of us. And he'd decided, very publicly, that he wasn't going anywhere.

This is not going to end well, I said to Luca, privately.

No, Luca agreed. *I have someone in mind to replace him, but they'll take convincing. For now, we'll let this stand.*

Outwardly, Luca shrugged, as if Brogan's acceptance meant absolutely nothing. Which, in my opinion, it did mean. Nothing.

"Good," Luca said. "You're all dismissed, then."

Absolutely no one left. They all stood up, they all meandered, but no one left.

Why? I whined, and Darkness, I'd already picked up the werewolf whine, even in my mental voice.

Welcome to pack leadership, Luca said grumpily, *where everyone can't wait to publicly kiss your ass and privately complain about how you're doing everything wrong.*

Great. Interesting as my sudden transformation to werewolf form had been, I decided it was time for it to be over. Having never been a wolf before, I felt like I might trip over my own paws at any moment, as having four feet simply did not feel natural for me. Oh, to be human again.

Once again, magic answered that thought and my body jerked, fur and fangs and claws receding as bones popped and rearranged themselves again. It *ought* to have hurt, but I wasn't going to complain about the fact that it didn't. I also wasn't going to complain about the fact that I'd just shifted from human to wolf and back and somehow, I wasn't naked.

My new clothes and all my weapons were fully present and accounted for.

"How did you do that?" Luca asked.

I shrugged. "It's good to be a Hunter-werewolf?" I suggested. I leaned over and plucked my Heartstone from the ground. Before the waves of pack sycophants descended on us, there was one thing I absolutely had to do.

I pressed my Heartstone to my chest. The jagged scar split open, welcoming the jewel back to where it belonged. And the second it settled, the second I felt my *true* power, not the shadow of it I'd been drawing on all this time, I felt a strange hooking sensation behind my navel, and the world dissolved into darkness.

When it came into focus once more, everyone except Luca was gone. And we stood in the center of Elysium's hexagram.

30

ASHLYNN

The daylight had vanished as if a giant had plucked the sun from the sky and swallowed it whole. The world lay silent and still and empty. Standing atop Elysium's hexagram, the sides of the valley sloping gently away from it, I felt as if Luca and I had been dropped into an abandoned sports stadium, the bleachers empty, the game long over.

We stood at one of the star's points, the white marble beneath our feet riddled with dark, like a mottled sickness upon the skin. And there, between the veins of black and white, was my name and Luca's.

"What the hell?" I said, softly. "Is this the Elders' idea of a joke?"

"I don't think they have a sense of humor," Luca replied grimly.

I couldn't shake a feeling of ancient loss, as if we stood upon the scene of some long-ago war, and all that had been left behind was cold sadness and the memories of spent lives.

"It was not quite a war." The melodic voice whirled through the valley like leaves caught in an autumn wind, a soft rustle and a sense of color that one couldn't see. It sounded like a memory. Or a figment of my imagination.

Luca? I asked silently, mind-to-mind. We stood back-to-back, rotating in a slow circle, scanning the area for potential threats.

I heard it.

I don't see anyone.

Laughter rippled through the air, sweet and chime-like. "I can *hear* you," the unknown stranger said in a singsong voice. "What you think, what you say."

I couldn't tell where the speaker came from. Their voice seemed to echo through the valley, coming from everywhere and nowhere at once.

"If it wasn't a war," I said, "what was it?" If I could just keep them talking, find out where that voice originated...

"It was a betrayal." As if to taunt me—and if the owner of the voice really *could* hear my thoughts, it no doubt *was* to taunt me—each of the four words sounded as if they came from a different point in the valley. "One that is still ongoing." This last sentence whispered in my ear. I could feel the lips that spoke it against my skin. But when I spun and slashed, knife in hand, I only cleaved through empty air, and that tinkling laughter sounded from far away.

"But what has been done can be undone," the voice said. "There is no magic death cannot break, no binding so permanent that leaving this world will not make it come apart."

"Big words from a disembodied voice who won't show herself," I shot back.

"Why show myself," the voice answered, "when I could show you *you?*" The last half of the sentence was spoken in *my* voice. My sound, my tone, my cadence. Me. As was the form that materialized in front of me. My height, my shape, my face—all made of solid shadow.

When Luca turned and stepped to my side, Shadow Me

tilted her head, considering. The air beside her wavered and a second shadow appeared. Luca.

I reached for my sword and Shadow Me did the same, pausing as I did, with her hand on the hilt.

I don't like this, Luca said.

Before I could answer, an echo of the words he'd spoken silently rumbled through the valley in Luca's voice.

I didn't like it any more than he did. I think, at the moment, I liked it less. But there was no point in telling him so, because apparently the Darkness was a damn mind-reader. That thought, in particular, seemed to amuse Shadow Me, because her form shook with laughter that filled the air.

"Let's get this over with." I slid the sword from its scabbard and struck even as Luca and Shadow Luca both sprouted fur and fangs and lunged at each other, quickly combining into a ball of fur and growls and snapping teeth that tumbled away from me and my own double.

I don't know what I had expected out of fighting a shadow version of myself that could read my mind, but it wasn't the precise copy of my movements that occurred. Every strike I made was met with its literal mirror.

In a true fight, one of the parties was aways reacting to the other. One person attacked, the other defended. Who was on the offensive or defensive could switch a dozen times, a fluid back-and-forth. The more skilled two fighters were, the more it might *look* like the fight was choreographed, but in truth, one half of everything was reactionary.

This—this felt precisely like choreography. It felt like doing the Meyer's Cross exercise for the German longsword. Meyer's Cross consisted of two people each performing the exact same four strikes, with one person advancing and the other retreating. Each strike from one person mirrored that of the other, and they could be repeated in an endless loop.

It looked pretty and far more complicated than it actually

was, and it was good to trot out as a flashy display to those uninitiated in the ways of bladed combat. The exercise was designed to help you work on fluidity and footwork, to get used to the feel of blade striking blade, and help you build up stamina, since the infinite-loop nature of it meant that if no one ever tired, it could be continued until the literal end of time.

Fighting Shadow Me—if I could even call what we were doing right now fighting—felt like doing Meyer's Cross. A pretty display that would never go anywhere, never result in a victory or loss.

I changed my approach, moved to strikes and advances that weren't in my typical repertoire, so to speak. It didn't make any difference. Because the issue wasn't that Shadow Me was good at countering my typical fighting style, it was that she knew my thoughts.

So I stopped thinking, and simply *did*. I didn't think about the fact that I was fighting what was, for all intents and purposes, *myself*. I lost myself in the meditative rise and fall of my sword, the block and parry, advance and retreat. Step and turn and strike. And this time, on that last turn, my double faltered, and my blade hit home.

❧ 31 ❧
LUCA

Fighting a fucked-up version of myself was the absolute last thing this day needed. In the past two hours I'd challenged my father, nearly been killed by him, gotten myself mated, my mate *had* killed my father, and then we'd finished the last requirement in a prophecy neither of us believed in, all so that fickle bitch called Fate could dump us *here*.

After dozens of failed attacks, in which my shadow wolf did exactly as I did, rage boiled over in me and I lost it. I gave myself over completely to the wolf, and let the animal do my thinking for me. The wolf wasn't concerned about right or wrong, fair or unfair. The wolf didn't care about prophecy or politics.

The wolf knew simply that he had reached his limit, that his mate was in danger and he couldn't get to her until this shadow was gone.

My human mind receded entirely. I became a flurry of teeth and claws and bloodlust. Somewhere amid that barrage of attacks, my copy faltered, and the wolf lunged. My teeth sank into the shadow wolf's throat. Bitter blood spilled onto my tongue, but I kept my hold, amazed that I *could*.

Before, every time I had fought anything wrought of Darkness, each bite, each swipe of claws, had hit nothing but mist. But it seemed Ashlynn's Heartstone had brought even more changes than I'd anticipated, had given me whatever it was about *her* that made her able to turn the Darkness corporeal, to kill the incarnation of it.

I bore the wolf to the ground, claws raking at the soft underbelly. Biting and rending until the form shuddered, went limp, and shattered, shadow reduced not to the body of a wolf, but to shards of silver glass.

I turned to Ashlynn, ready to leap to her aid, but she didn't need my help. She fought like the Hunter she was, all fluidity and grace, muscles trained for swordplay carrying out their purpose. Her copy suffered from dozens of gashes, but the cuts didn't bleed—at least, not in the traditional sense. They bled *light*, pure silver rays piercing the dark with such brilliance it was almost blinding to look at.

The shadow struck. Ash dodged, pivoted, and struck low across the shadow's achilles tendon. Ash's double fell to her knees, more light than shadow now, and her entire body began to vibrate. The shadow shook and trembled, faster and faster, until—as my own copy had—her body fractured into pieces with a sound like breaking glass.

Shards of her rained down on the hexagram floor, clattering against each other like divining bones. The pieces of the shadow I'd destroyed began to rattle, as if an earthquake shook the stone hexagram, and they moved to join the pieces of Ash's shadow. The two swirled about each other, melted to liquid and condensed before clattering to the stone once more, a new shape formed.

I shifted back to human and walked with Ash to the silver piece on the ground that was all that was left of the creatures we'd fought. It was a long cylinder the length of my hand, with one flat rectangular piece descending from each end at ninety-degree angles.

"Is that part of a key?" Ash asked. It sat in the exact center of the hexagram, and now that she pointed out the obvious, it did look like the end of an old-fashioned key. A very *large* key.

Before she could answer, I sensed movement to our left. The veins of black that had mottled the point of the star where our names were etched began to writhe. They slid from the point, into the center of the hexagram, and coalesced into a black rectangle on the stone.

My eyebrows lifted. "Is that the start of a keyhole?"

"What the fuck, Luca?"

"I don't know."

"Is this a game? Are the Elders playing a goddamn fucking game with us?"

"Even a game," whispered a voice, similar to the one that had spoken initially, but deeper, lower, "can have very real consequences. Take the piece. You've earned it. And don't panic. The separation from the others is necessary."

Separation? From what *others?* Ash's hand slid into mine while we eyed the piece of key—or whatever it was —sidelong.

What do you say we break for the hills? Ash suggested. *Bet I can beat you back to White Woods.*

I *felt* someone listening to the thoughts, even as wind swept through the valley like a sigh and blew the piece that might or might not be a key to Ash's feet. As soon as it touched the tip of her boot, the world dissolved again.

We appeared in the pack clearing, right where we'd left from. The key piece landed between Ash's feet with a clatter. We had less than half a second of peace before loud, anxious werewolves descended on us. Through the chaotic chatter, I caught one thing, repeated over and over again.

"We can't get out."

I pulled on the pack bonds, on the magic that linked Ash and I, alphas to pack, and said, "Everyone calm down."

The cacophony of noise and energy quieted, stilled. I searched the pack until I found Gareth. "What's going on?"

"We were hoping you could tell us. You disappeared. Then the White Woods borders closed."

"What do you mean they closed?"

"I mean that none of us can leave pack territory—and no one else can enter."

I remembered that damn voice saying, *The separation from the others is necessary,* and cursed. Silently, because I was now in charge of this pack. I also resisted the desire to pinch the bridge of my nose for the same reason.

Aloud, I just said, "Okay. Gareth, you come with me and Ash, we'll run the perimeter—"

"We've already done that," Brogan cut in. Then added, "Alpha," as an afterthought.

I fixed Brogan with a hard stare. It had nothing on the one Ash leveled him with, if the intensity radiating off her was any indication. I needed to shut this down, fast.

I had no doubt Brogan had used our disappearance to immediately start sowing pack discord. I needed to handle this—both the blatant disrespect he'd just shown and the pack's fear at being trapped inside White Woods—before it had time to foment.

I could call on the pack bonds to *make* Brogan submit, but doing that wouldn't fix his attitude, or convince the pack that I could lead them. I'd spent the last twelve years blatantly flaunting my intention *not* to lead them. I knew the pack politics inside and out because Gareth had insisted on keeping me apprised of them over the years, because he'd insisted that I was going to end up right where I was now.

He was going to be an insufferable prick about being

right, but the joke would be on him, in the end. Because Brogan needed replacing, and Gareth was just the wolf to do it.

"Beta," I said, making the rank sound like an insult. "I have no doubt you've run the perimeter, as only an idiot would have failed to." Brogan's sharp intake of breath was music to my ears. If I got lucky, he'd lose his shit and challenge me, and we could be done with this stupid mess. Unfortunately, he got a grip on himself and stayed right where he was.

"However, *Ash and I* have not run the perimeter." It was a statement with a twofold purpose. One, it showed we cared enough to do the investigation ourselves. Two, it implied a lack of trust in his own reconnaissance. "Do you have some objection to your alphas taking a personal interest in the pack's current situation?"

Brogan gave the only response he could, with the question framed like that. "No, Alpha."

"Good. Then Ash, Gareth, and I will run the perimeter. While we are gone, you will take a thorough census of the pack. I want every member accounted for. If anyone was outside of the White Woods border when it closed, I want to know about it."

❦ 32 ❦

ASHLYNN

A WALL OF OPAQUE WHITE MIST HAD SPRUNG UP AROUND the perimeter of the White Woods territory, seamless and impenetrable. As I watched, the edges seemed to shift and swirl, but if I pressed my hand to it, it felt like smooth, cool glass, solid and impenetrable.

If there was an obvious means of getting through, we didn't find it.

Two brand new alphas explaining to a literal pack of angry wolves that we were all trapped within our own territory for "we don't know how long" and "we don't know why," went about as well as could be expected.

But though life in the mortal world had made me think I would never use my childhood instruction, I *had* been raised to lead. And if Luca and I were going to do this, if this was going to be my life, I wanted to do it well.

It wasn't as if I suddenly had warm fuzzy feelings for the pack as a whole—they'd still let Luca's father chain him in silver when he was just a kid, hadn't said a word about the Elders throwing me and the other five away when it was convenient for them. But I was stuck on this island with them regardless, and now I was stuck in this territory with them.

And if I was being honest with myself, the Elders hadn't given anyone much of a chance to object to my banishment all those years ago. It had been less than a handful of hours between the Oracle's prophecy and the Elders' actions, which wasn't a lot of time for anyone to mount a defense, had they wanted to. It didn't mean I held them blameless. I still felt that people should have done something, at least *said* something, when I was dragged past them on the streets, but I could understand, to some degree, how it might have taken everyone by surprise.

Crowd mentality is a hard thing to break through. Everyone wants to believe they would be the person who would make the right choice, the moral choice, when everything around them is going to hell, but the truth is, most people don't. The movies make it look easy to be the one person in a thousand who steps forward to defend someone who deserves it, but history is riddled with the opposite.

It doesn't make the silence of those who know better *right*, but I'd like to think that maybe those who'd sat by back then and wished for the bravery to act would do so the next time they found themselves in a similar situation.

And where individual growth didn't happen on its own, society was supposed to be there to enforce the correct decision. As newly-minted alphas Luca and I were, for all intents and purposes, werewolf society. So I tamped down on over a decade's worth of bitterness, and I *led*.

I calmed panicked werewolves. I listened to the same fears and complaints over and over, and I gave the same responses, over and over.

Yes, it was likely that the barrier was related to the

prophecy. No, we didn't know how long it would last. Yes, the pack territory had resources and provisions enough to last six months (thank you, Gareth, for knowing that information).

If it appeared this magical barrier was going to last for longer than that, we were going to be in trouble. The last thing I wanted was to be trapped in a relatively small area with a bunch of people notorious for having anger management issues and killing each other to solve their disagreements.

But for now, people were calmed simply by the fact that Luca and I, prophecy-named fated mates—and dear sweet mortals' Jesus, I was never *not* going to snarl when I thought of that—were not freaking out, and by the fact that all of our wolves were accounted for within the territory. I had no idea how we'd gotten that lucky.

Even that might not have been enough to quell a true panic if the necessity of checking in on every wolf in the territory hadn't brought to light another discovery. Without exception, every wolf that had had Darksickness prior to Luca and I's fight in the hexagram had recovered.

I wondered if that effect had spread through the whole island, or if it was just our now-isolated territory. Had my father recovered, or was he going to die while I waited behind walls of white mist and co-led the people he'd once told me to leave?

"Copper for you thoughts?" Luca asked, his voice rough but soft. We were walking back to his cabin, having stationed guards at each of the roads that led out of the White Woods, on the off chance someone came through from the other side. Or, you know, in case if someone was standing on the other side shouting their lungs out and sound could travel through the barrier, we would hear it.

But given the fact I now had werewolf hearing and I

couldn't hear the wind on the other side of the barrier, or smell anything past it, I doubted we could talk to anyone even if they were standing a foot away from us.

"It's nothing," I said. I wasn't going to talk about my father when I'd just killed Luca's hours ago. I tried to think of something else to say for when he inevitably pushed—Luca *always* pushed—but all that came out of him in reply was a noncommittal noise.

It brought to the forefront the issue I'd personally been avoiding. Somewhere in the middle of the stress of dealing with the territory's closed borders and the attendant mess that came with pack change of leadership, Luca's feelings— my awareness of him through the bond—had gone muted. Like he didn't want me to know what he felt, and he was somehow dampening the transferral.

I didn't know what that meant. Was he upset that I'd killed Aiden? Yes, the man had tried to kill Luca, but he had still been his father.

Could he be upset about the mating bond? The Heartstones? He'd *wanted* to be mated to me—I'd felt that, known that, but maybe he'd only wanted that in the aftermath of emotions he'd felt when Clay had tried to force me. Maybe it had just been protectiveness and temporary possessiveness.

He'd said he loved me, but love and a mating bond were different things. Maybe he'd had time to think about it, and decided being mated wasn't what he wanted. And I'd just done it anyway, without asking him, without even giving him any warning.

And our Heartstones...I hadn't asked him about *that* either. The mating bond, at least, had seemed like an open offer, and he *had* already joined his Heartstone to mine, but still, I hadn't asked before I'd done either. Hadn't given him any warning.

We trudged up the cabin steps. Inside, behind the safety of closed doors and soundproofed walls, I'd hoped he would let up on the vice grip he had on his emotions. But if anything, he clamped down even harder, until my awareness of him through the bond dwindled to practically nothing.

The only thing I felt coming off him from our joined Heartstones was turmoil and regret. If there were other emotions beneath them, those two were strong enough they drowned out everything else, and it turned my insides to knots.

Especially when he turned away from me without a word, went into the kitchen and pulled down a bottle of whiskey and two glasses. He splashed a healthy amount into one, knocked it back in a single gulp, then filled both glasses with a more than generous serving.

Shit.

I caught the glass he slid across the counter while he stared at me like I was a viper that might strike at any moment.

He'd said he loved me. I'd *felt* that he loved me. But that had been before...everything. Before mating and Heartstones and joint alphas.

Was it the last thing that had done it? Did he not want me to lead the pack with him? Undoubtedly, my being in co-charge would make everything more difficult for him. Even given my new wolf form, it would take time—years, probably—before the pack truly accepted me as one of them. If they ever did.

Did he want me to step aside? If he did—if he asked me—I would. But it would hurt. My father had already given me a vote of no-confidence for the territory I had been born to lead. If Luca gave me one for the territory I'd *chosen* to lead...I didn't know what that would do to our relationship. If we would still have a relationship after that, if he even *wanted* to still have a relationship.

I didn't want to lose my best friend. Not when I'd just gotten him back. I took a swallow of whiskey, then decided Luca had had the right of it and finished the rest. It burned down my throat, hit my stomach with a harsh flare of warmth.

"Are you pissed at me?" I blurted out. That was me, Ashlynn Hunter, eloquent to the core.

He looked at me like I was an idiot. So that was a yes, then, of course he was pissed at me, because—

"Why the hell would I be mad at you?"

"Because I killed your father? Because I took the mating bond and forced my Heartstone on you without asking about either?" Fuck, when I put it that way, the enormity of every decision I'd made today slammed into me. The first couldn't be undone at all, and the last two not without one of us dying. Even that might not undo a Heartstone joining. Myth held that if Luca died, the half of my Heart I had given to him would die with him, and the half of his he had given to me would live on with me.

I couldn't decide if that was romantic or disturbing.

"Ash, if I'd been smarter, *I* would have killed my father, yield or no. The mating bond was yours to take, and as for the Heartstones, I gave you mine without asking. We can sit around all day wondering if we both did the wrong thing, or we can accept the truth."

"And what's that?" I asked softly.

His hand stretched across the counter for mine and our fingers twined together. "We were always going to be together, baby. Not because some stupid prophecy said it, not because the Elders wanted it. But because we're the same. Because my heart *is* your heart, and it was from the moment I met you."

"Then what's the problem?" I asked. "Why did you shut me out? Why does it feel like you think this is ending?"

"Because I'm worried it will." His thumb stroked across the back of my hand. "I know this isn't what you wanted, Ash. The mating bond, the Heartstones, the prophecy. Leading the pack."

I inhaled sharply, wondering if now was when he would tell me that he didn't think both of us leading the pack was a good idea.

"It's a fucking lot to put on a person and it's my fault. I knew Dad wouldn't give up the alpha position without something underhanded, but I never expected a silver knife. I thought he'd shift again as soon as I turned my back on him.

"If I'd anticipated it, if I'd been smarter, you never would have been put in this position."

I blinked. "*That's* what had you all morose? You thought I'd be upset I ended up co-alpha?"

"You're not?"

I thought about it, because he deserved an honest answer. "One, it's not your fault your father was a cowardly asshole, so if I *was* upset, it wouldn't be at you. Two—no, I'm not unhappy. You always came with the pack as baggage. Whether *you* admitted or not, you were always going to be alpha some day.

"And as you pointed out," I continued, lifting his hand to press a kiss to his palm, "you were always going to be mine. So I'd be dealing with the pack's bullshit whether or not I also carried the alpha title. Having it just makes dealing with them a little easier.

"And I think—" I hesitated, not sure what he would think of what I was about to say. But we were partners now. In more ways than one. We had to be comfortable being honest at some point. "I think the pack could use us.

"I wouldn't blame you if you hated the lot of them and left them to their own devices to become the most unavailable pack alpha in history. But I think part of the way they act comes from a history of bad leadership. I think we could do some good here, Luca. For everyone."

Luca leaned across the counter and kissed me, long and hard. "So do I."

Breathless and reeling from the kiss, it took me a minute to make sure I'd heard right. "You do?"

"My father isn't the only person who failed this pack, Ash. I did too. Maybe I had good reasons for hiding here in the outskirts for the last twelve years, but that's exactly what I was doing. Hiding.

"Darkness knows I blame them for not even flinching when they walked past me when I was chained to the Elder Tree, but even I know how hard it was to defy Aiden when he was alpha. I should have challenged him years ago."

"Why didn't you?"

He was quiet for a minute, and then he said, "I didn't think I deserved it. I was physically strong enough to beat Aiden, but all I felt was weak. I failed to protect you, to protect my sister, when the elders banished you. Who I was to lead the pack when I couldn't even save the two most important people in my life?"

My heart broke for him, knowing he'd felt that way. Knowing I'd blamed him for years for something both of us had been too young to stop. "You were fifteen, Luca."

He gave me a bitter half-smile. "I get that, now. But it's hard to separate who you are now from who you were then, you know? It took leaving, finding you, to make me realize that." He ran his hands over his face. "And now I have to live with the fact that I let people endure him for the last decade."

"That isn't all on you, Luca. Maybe you didn't challenge him, but no one else did either."

I waited for him to tell me that of course no one else had, because no one else had had a chance of beating Aiden. Interestingly, he just said, "That's true."

Which made me wonder. "Who did you have in mind for beta?" As if I didn't already know. Because if there was someone in the pack strong enough to beat Aiden *other* than Luca, it would have to be someone who had very determinedly stayed out of pack power struggles their entire life. Say, a certain redheaded wolf who refused to ever engage in fights.

"You know exactly who I have in mind."

"I don't think Gareth's interested in being pack beta."

Luca rolled his eyes. "Who the hell knows what Gareth's actually interested in?"

I did. Her name started with a K, and after her throwing her weight behind me in front of the pack today, I no longer knew what to make of her.

"It's time he did something himself after badgering me to for years. Do you agree with the choice?"

"What would you do if I didn't?"

"Take your counter-suggestion and make my own arguments in Gareth's favor. Not make a decision until we agreed."

The answer sent a warmth through me that the whiskey couldn't match. I might be alpha where the pack bonds were concerned, but I knew damn well that if Luca didn't treat me as his equal, the pack wouldn't either. If he wanted to make decisions without me, he could. And I was so, so glad that I'd judged him right. That he respected me the way I needed him to.

"I'm fine with Gareth." I drummed my fingers on the counter, trying to decide if I should say anything else.

"But?" Luca prompted.

"But I think he's in a delicate place right now."

Luca's eyebrows crept up. "I wouldn't say 'delicate.' Temperamental for sure. He'll settle down once he has a job to do."

"I don't think it's that simple. And I think, if he's going to work with us, the two of you have something you need to sort out."

Luca frowned. "I don't have any issues with Gareth."

"I'm aware."

"You're saying he has one with me? What did I do?"

I sighed. "It's really not my place to say. And you didn't do anything *wrong*, necessarily—"

"Are you going to tell me what it is?"

"I can't. Just talk to him, okay? Promise me you'll get it sorted out?"

I could see he wanted to push. Luca was like a dog with a bone—pun totally intended—when someone else knew something he wanted to know. But spilling other people's personal anguish was so not something I had a right to do. Gareth was my friend, too, and I wouldn't betray his confidence.

I slipped around the counter, wrapped my arms around Luca's waist, and kissed him. "Promise me you'll talk to him," I prompted. I slid my hands under his shirt, ran them up the muscles of his back and saw his eyes light up with lust. Cheating? Probably.

"Whatever you say, Alpha," Luca agreed, lowering his mouth to nip his way down my neck.

"If you start calling me 'Alpha' in bed, how am I ever going to look the pack in the eye when they call me that?"

He grinned and ripped my shirt off. Literally. It was a waste of a brand new shirt. It was also maddeningly hot.

"Sounds like your problem to me." His hands roved over

my stomach, skated up my ribs to cup my breasts. I moaned and arched into the touch.

We had more to discuss, more to figure out. How we would lead the pack, what changes we wanted to make. What to do about White Woods' sudden isolation. But as Luca's lips trailed down, as he peeled the cup of my bra aside and took my nipple in his mouth, I was very aware that we didn't have to make those decisions *right* now.

Luca's hand delved into my pants, his fingers parting the folds between my legs, where I was already hot and wet.

"Luca?"

"Yes, my love?"

"Is it true what they say about the mating bond and sex? That you can feel what the other person feels?"

He gave me a wicked grin and all of his emotions, everything he'd clamped down on from the mating bond, roared into me. "Give it back to me, baby, and let's find out."

I opened myself to him, let everything I felt for him pour through the bond. His mouth met mine, claimed it in a rough tangle of tongues. Heat and lust were a fire raging through me, but it wasn't just *mine*, my need, my desire. It was Luca's, too.

And Darkness, he wanted me.

I jumped him, wrapped my legs around his waist and felt the rock hard length of his cock press against my core. Felt what *he* felt as I ground against his erection, as his want skyrocketed and his dick throbbed in response.

I raked my fingernails up his back. The points shifted to claws and I stilled, fighting to control the beast inside me that suddenly want to shift and run wild. I wasn't used to having to deny the wolf when my passions ran hot.

"Don't hold yourself back, baby." Luca turned and pinned me to the wall. "A little shift is normal. You won't go all the way."

His confidence, his lack of concern, was enough to quell the change, claws retracting back to human fingers. I tore his shirt off, unhooked my legs and slid down his body to undo his pants. He sprang free into my hand, massive and gloriously hard, and I put my mouth where I'd wanted it for days.

He groaned when I took him, his fingers biting into my shoulders, and I felt every exquisite sensation he did when I swirled my tongue around his head, teased gently at his slit. He was already leaking pre-come and I drank the salty drops down, felt how good it was for him when I swallowed around his shaft.

I began to suck him in earnest, cupped his tight balls in my hand and gently squeezed. I felt the reverberations of my work, knew just what pace to strike to drive him right to the edge of madness. So I did. And when he would have pulled back I gripped his hips and held him, moved on him until he lost restraint and fucked my mouth like he wanted to.

And as I felt his pleasure build and build I took him him fully and he came with a shuddering roar, spilling down the back of my throat. I swallowed his come down, then eased him gently out of my mouth.

He grabbed my arms and pulled me to my feet, his eyes blazing. "Take your clothes off."

I did as ordered, unhooked my bra and shimmied out of pants and underwear. His hands gripped my ass, squeezed, and lifted me onto the counter. He nudged my knees wide, baring my pussy, his gaze hot and full of want.

I was embarrassingly wet. He stroked a finger through the slick folds and my hips jerked forward, needing more. His other hand came up and pinned my hips, holding me down.

"You liked sucking me," he said, "liked making me come. I felt it."

It wasn't a question, but I answered it anyway. "Yes."

"You liked it when I lost control and fucked your mouth."

He punctuated the rough statement by flicking his thumb across my clit. I tried to follow, needing that touch again, but his hand on my hip prevented me.

"I loved it," I answered.

"Feel how much I love this," he said. He threw my legs over his shoulders and lowered his mouth to my pussy, his tongue dragging a wide line up my center.

I cried out and bucked against him. His hands came under my ass, kneading my flesh, rocking me against him as his mouth devoured me. He worked me expertly, feeling everything I felt, knowing just when to circle my clit with his tongue, to suck me into his mouth, when I wanted his fingers inside me.

He thrust and licked and sucked until I couldn't think, couldn't breathe, until I was so close to the edge I thought I would die if I didn't come. His fingers plunged into me again, his hand on my ass pulling me hard against his mouth. He rolled my clit between his teeth and all the building pressure in me exploded.

I screamed, arching into him, my thighs clamping hard around his face as I rode wave after wave of ecstasy. I was barely cognizant as he picked me up and carried me to his bedroom. He set me on my feet, the prominent press of his erection against me starting the cycle of need all over again.

"Turn around."

Darkness, yes. I turned around and bent over, bracing my hands on the bed and baring myself to him. He ran his hands up my thighs, over my ass. "You are so fucking gorgeous," he growled.

The blunt head of his cock pressed against my entrance and I whimpered in anticipation. "You know what I want," I told him. It was there between us, in the bond, that understanding of each other's desires.

"I know." He ran his hands over the small of my back,

then down to grip my hips. I readied myself, tilting my ass up to welcome him.

Without warning, he impaled himself in me fully in one single, brutal thrust. He was so deep in me, stretching me so fully, but it wasn't enough. I backed up on him, feeling my ass against his stomach, his balls against my thighs.

He groaned, his fingers digging into me. "Do you feel how tight you are on my cock?" he asked roughly. "How sweet your pussy is?"

I couldn't articulate words. I did. I felt all of that and more from him, but hearing him say it, put it into words, was erotic beyond imagining.

"Tell me what you want, baby." His hands slid over my stomach, came up to cup my breasts. He rolled my nipples between his fingers and I moaned. I backed against him again, needing movement, needing more of him. "Tell me, baby. Say it." He punctuated the demand by squeezing my breasts, his hands rough and demanding, but I was too much a raging tangle of need to form words.

He withdrew until only the tip of him nudged my entrance, and I was barren for lack of him. His hands came back to my ass, kneading and spreading me wide, and I found the words to tell him what I wanted. "Fuck me, Luca. Hard and fast."

He slammed into me so hard I'd swear the entire room shook.

"Again," I demanded. I needed more, needed more of him, *now*. He pulled out and returned, the friction of his big cock ecstasy as he moved in and out of my channel. I reached my hand between my legs, not for my clit, not immediately, but to place my fingers to feel his shaft, slick with my desire, each time he withdrew.

He groaned and began to fuck me in earnest, each thrust making me crave the next as he hit home. The ache at the apex of my thighs grew unbearable and my fingers found my clit, working desperate little circles. I panted, gasped for breath as the twin sensations of my fingers on the center of my pleasure and Luca's cock penetrating my core pushed me to the edge...and then over it.

I came with a harsh cry, every muscle in my pussy clamping down on Luca's cock. I felt it as *he* felt it, felt my orgasm obliterate the last shreds of his control. His hands on my hips pulled me hard against him each time he drove in, once more, twice, the echoes of my orgasm milking his shaft.

He barreled into my depths one final time and came with a guttural growl, his release an explosion of heat as he spilled himself into me.

I sagged onto the bed, barely able to keep my legs from going out. Luca wasn't much better off, draped over my back, still buried in me. He nuzzled the side of my neck, pressed a kiss to the junction of my collarbone.

"I think you're going to be the death of me, Ashlynn Hunter," he murmured.

I smiled into the mattress. "What's the matter, Prince Snowflake? Never been fucked until you can't stand up before?"

"As a matter of fact, no." He pulled out of me, wrapped his arms around my waist and tumbled us onto the bed. My ass wedged against his cock, which was doing its level best to show interest again. "However, I have every intention of repeating the experience. Possibly every day for the rest of my life, if my mate is willing."

"I might be willing." I rolled over to face him. "If you're a very good wolf, and say, 'Pretty please, Alpha.'"

"I love it when you're demanding." He took my mouth in a long, sensual kiss. "I love *you*, Ash."

"And I love you, Luca Ferrar." I kissed him back, lost

myself in the taste and feel of him, and knew that, from then on, I would never be alone again.

Things were a mess, and the pack would always be difficult. But I had Luca, and he had me, and that was all we needed.

EPILOGUE
DEVRYN RYDER

I STOOD AT THE BORDER BETWEEN ELYSIUM CENTRAL AND White Woods, looking at the wall of white mist that had sprung up between the two territories. I wasn't entirely sure when it had appeared. My focus had been elsewhere, on the hexagram in Elysium's central valley, which an hour ago had suddenly become shrouded in darkness.

I had no doubt Luca and Ashlynn had been in the center of that darkness, but neither I nor anyone else had been able to penetrate the darkness to find out. Not that many had tried. Only the current territory heirs had even bothered to investigate.

After trying futilely for an hour to break through to the hexagram, the darkness had simply vanished. Everything had gone back to normal, except the hexagram was empty, save that one of the star points was cleared of corruption, and now bore Luca's and Ashlynn's names.

It wasn't long after that before Renna and Brendan, my second and third in command, had appeared to report that the border to White Woods was closed. The Siren territory bordered White Woods on the other side, and the Siren heir had received a similar report before Renna had even finished giving hers.

Now we were all standing at the White Woods border, five prickly territory heirs who didn't like being so close in each others' company, even if we *were* on neutral ground. The only thing we had in common, aside from one day inheriting rule, was that the people currently ruling our territories couldn't be bothered to investigate this strange occurrence themselves.

"No one can get through?" I asked Renna, even though I already knew the answer.

"It's impassable from any approach," she answered. Her gaze slipped to the Faerie prince, Mavrien Hevera, as if she expected him to attack at any moment. Which was...odd. Faerie and Hunter weren't exactly friendly, but we'd been in an ice-cold, no blood-shedding truce for as long as I'd been alive.

"Maybe a *Hunter* can't get through." Benedict's voice dripped with the arrogance all Dragons seemed to be gifted upon entering the world.

Mavrien swept a cold gaze over the dragon heir. "By all means then, Benedict, do show us lesser beings how it is done." The two stared at each other, locked in some unspoken contest. Four silver scars snaked down the Fae prince's face, scars he'd acquired in childhood that looked an exact match for a Dragon's claws. Despite how much Elysians liked to gossip, I'd never heard a whisper of how those scars had come to be.

I thought we might all age into stone before the two of them broke out of their staring contest. Then Benedict grinned, a flashing of teeth that was more baring of fangs than friendly gesture, and exhaled a stream of smoke. "I'd be delighted to."

The heat radiating from his body practically singed my

skin as he stomped past—Dragons were *forever* stomping everywhere they went—and came to a stop at the mist wall surrounding White Woods.

He inhaled deeply, the air around him shimmering with heat. Then he open his mouth and roared, a torrent of white-hot flame jetting at the boundary. Dragons were impressive and flashy, I'd give them that. But they were also at a complete loss any time fire or brute strength didn't solve a problem.

The look on Benedict's face when Dragon fire didn't bring the mist wall down in a pile of crumbling ash was comical. He tried three or four more times, until his body itself was a glowing ember, burning with flame.

Mavrien stepped right up next to the enraged Dragon. Which should have been impossible. A Dragon who had been breathing fire for upwards of five minutes was basically a raging inferno. The Fae prince should be a mess of blistering skin on the verge of death.

My second looked a little dejected, as if she'd hoped Mavrien *would* be burnt to a crisp. I would say that was just Renna's intense personal dislike of the Fae, a hatred I'd never learned the origins of, but the glances she'd been giving the Fae prince had been more wary and speculative than born of simple animosity.

Mavrien stood unharmed, looking cool as fresh winter snow, and clapped Benedict on the shoulder. "Feeling under the weather, Benny?"

Benedict turned with a snarl on his lips, his eyes two glowing embers. He didn't look surprised that Mavrien hadn't keeled over dead, and that was...interesting. Just when I thought he would lose it and start a territory war, Benedict blinked, the fire in his eyes flickering out, and the temperature dropped to a more livable level. "The boundary appears to be impervious to Dragon fire."

No shit. But I didn't say that out loud. Unlike Mavrien, I didn't have a death wish.

"It is also impassable from above." Zephyr, the Icarii prince, landed gracefully, tucking in the six-foot span of blue wings that had given the mortals their legends of angels. "I've flown over the entire territory."

The Hunters, the Dragons, and the Icarii had all struck out. We turned expectantly to Mavrien and Tristan.

"I'm afraid the land doesn't speak to me here," Mavrien said, as if the entire endeavor was beneath him. "The Fae won't be burrowing under this border." He turned to Tristan, the Siren heir. "Well, we've all given it our best shot. Going to sing it open for us?"

Tristan rolled his eyes, but power coalesced in the air around him. When he opened his mouth, what came out was not a song in the traditional way one thought of them. It was music, yes, and beauty, but it was wordless, born not of instruments but of the world and emotion, as if the wind and the water and the land all answered his call and wove themselves into the manifestation of his desire.

That song teased at the mist wall's edges, coaxing and enticing. The mist swirled, as if it was indeed enticed. I wasn't sure how much time passed as Tristan continued to sing power until sweat broke out on his face.

The wall shuddered. The tone of Tristan's song changed, hitting a higher, more insistent key. A tiny, near infinitesimal crack opened in the wall's facade. It held for a fraction of a second before the wall lashed out, retaliating with a wave of mist that sealed the crack and struck at Tristan like a tidal wave.

His song broke and he dropped to one knee, his magic utterly spent. No one had any wisecracks for the Siren after that. He'd gotten further than any of the rest of us, after all.

Renna, after shooting another subtle, gauging glance at

Mavrien, said, "Devryn, if all that can be done here has been done, there are matters in Hunter that require your attention."

I got her message loud and clear. She wanted us to leave. Now. My second always had a good reason for everything she did, and right now I was guessing that reason had something to do with the Faerie prince, even if it was beyond me to think of what that reason could be.

Since none of the territory heirs were keen on being in each others' presence longer than necessary, it didn't take much conversing for us all to agree to send this problem to the Elders and wait for further action.

Renna, Brendan and I were barely into Hunter territory when I stopped and rounded on them. "All right, what is it?"

They shared a glance, as if the two people I trusted most in all of Hunter were afraid I was going to bite one of their heads off after they spoke.

"Just spit it out," I said.

"It's the Oracle," Renna said finally. "He claims it's time for the next of the Six to return. It's Brialyn. From the Fae territory."

A sharp twinge went through me. Before the banishment, before Barren Hunter had chosen me to replace Ashlynn, Brialyn Hevera had been the one bright spot in my miserable life. And I'd only seen her once, the pretty, Fae princess with silver hair and lavender eyes. And if I'd known who she was then, I'd never have approached her.

But I hadn't known when I'd first laid eyes on her down by the Halcyon River, at the place where it left Faerie and entered Hunter lands. She'd been sitting on a rock, her bare feet in the water, picking at a plate of artfully arranged food like it had offended her. It was more food than I'd had in the past three days, and she'd been so small and quiet that it had occurred to me to steal it from her.

Then she'd looked up. Those lavender eyes had bored straight into mine, and I'd recognized a kindred spirit. I hadn't known how or why, but I'd known in my core that here was someone who would understand me. Someone I could trust. A friend.

So even though it would have been so easy to knock her over, steal that plate and finally curb the constant hunger in my stomach, I hadn't. To this day, I couldn't tell you how long we stared at each other before she'd stood, daintily pulling her feet from the water.

She'd never dropped my gaze before pointedly sliding the plate and all its contents over the invisible line that separated Faerie from Hunter. Then she'd just turned and walked away.

I'd yelled after her, unsure why I cared about anything other than the food she'd left. "Will you come back?" I'd asked.

She'd stopped, turned and raised an eyebrow in a mannerism that looked like it belonged on a forty-year-old, not a kid. "Do you want *me* to come back, or the food?"

"You," I'd said, completely honest.

"All right," she'd said. She hesitated, then, "If I can, I'll see you tomorrow."

She hadn't told me her name, and I hadn't told her mine. I had never gone back. Because the next day the Oracle had spoken, the Six had been banished, and Barren Hunter had kept my days too busy for me to escape to the river.

Even so, I'd held on to the memory of her, of that connection I'd felt when I'd looked into her eyes. I'd wondered if she *had* come back to the river to meet me, and if she ever wondered why I hadn't. It wasn't until years later, when I'd met Mavrien, his face such a mirror of *hers,* the same silver hair and lavender eyes, that I'd understood she had never gone back to the river. That she never *would* go back to the river. That she'd been lost to the mortal realm.

I'd realized then that the stupid fantasy I'd held on to over the years, of imagining the woman she would have grown into, of imagining a time when Barren Hunter was dead and I would finally be free to take one miserable hour to myself to venture into Faerie and *find* her, would never be anything more than a fantasy.

"Dev?" Brendan said softly, snapping me out of memory. Brendan and Renna were staring at me expectantly.

"What does that have to do with me?" I asked. I'd never told anyone about the girl by the river. And once I'd figured out who she was, I'd been glad of the fact.

"The Oracle announced who it is that's to go find her." Brendan shuffled his feet. I'd never seen him this off-balance, this weird.

I told myself it didn't mean anything, even though a flame of hope had stupidly kindled to life inside me. Because when the Oracle had made his damn prophecies, when I'd known Brialyn was coming home, an idiotic part of me had hoped beyond all reason that I would be the one to bring her back.

I'd told myself it was stupid. I'd met her all of once, had barely spoken to her. And she—she probably didn't even remember me. Some half-starved kid she'd taken a moment's pity on. But I remembered her, and I always would.

Hope kindled in my chest. If I was the one to go after Brialyn, it would explain her desire to get me away from Mavrien before he found out. Who knew how the Fae prince would react to that news. The Fae could be...territorial.

"It's—" Brendan started, stopped. "The thing is, Dev, the Oracle named *you*."

The grin that broke out on my face must have confused the hell out of my second and third, if the looks on their faces were any indication. I didn't care, *couldn't* care, couldn't even hear anything else they said past the pounding of my heart in my ears.

Brialyn Hevera was finally coming home. And I was going to be the one to bring her back.

ABOUT THE AUTHOR

S.M. Shadow writes steamy paranormal and fantasy romance novels, and urban fantasy with a strong romantic subplot.

She loves bad action movies, medieval weaponry, and cold weather. She drinks too much coffee, tea, and alcohol, and if she had to eat only one thing for the rest of her life, it would be sushi.

She thinks you're awesome for taking the time out of your life to read her bio, and hopes you're having a great day.

You can find her on her website: https://smshadow.com or follow her on Facebook.